To Jack,

'Always live the adventure.'

Christopher J Albert

ONLY
THE
BRAVE
DARE

CHRISTOPHER J. HOLCROFT

ISBN 978-0-7414-6994-6 Paperback
ISBN 978-0-7414-6995-3 eBook

Printed in the United States of America

Published December 2011

First published in 2008 by Poseidon Books
An imprint of Zeus Publications
P.O. Box 2554,
Burleigh M.D.C. QLD. 4220
Australia

The National Library of Australia Cataloguing-in-Publication
ISBN 978-1-921406-14-0 (pbk.)
I. Title.
A823.4

INFINITY PUBLISHING
1094 New DeHaven Street, Suite 100
West Conshohocken, PA 19428-2713
Toll-free (877) BUY BOOK
Local Phone (610) 941-9999
Fax (610) 941-9959
Info@buybooksontheweb.com
www.buybooksontheweb.com

Books written by Christopher J. Holcroft:

'*The novel is definitely a decent, educational experience for any teenager.*'

Venturer Chris Gantert

'*A fast paced adventure story, this will appeal to boys who are in the Scouting movement and the descriptions of the advantages of being a Venturer would perhaps encourage young boys to join the group.*'

Pat Pledger – ReadPlus

To my wife Yvonne, for all the love she gives me.

*To Venturers and Explorer Scouts everywhere ...
extend yourself and meet the challenges that confront
you.*

ABOUT THE AUTHOR

Christopher Holcroft's background is in communications; media training, complex public information planning and implementation, effective design of major community relations projects and journalism.

Since 1974, Christopher has been an active member of the Army Reserve. Christopher's deployments have included Bougainville onboard *HMAS Tobruk* in 1999 to instruct members of the United Nations-sponsored Peace Monitoring Group. In 2001 he acted as the Senior Military Public Affairs Adviser in East Timor for the Australian National Command Element of the United Nations Transitional Authority East Timor (UNTAET).

In 2006, Christopher was appointed the Senior Military Public Affairs Officer for the Middle East and was based in Baghdad, Iraq. He worked for the Australian Headquarters of Joint Task Force 633.

Christopher was awarded the Reserve Forces Decoration (RFD) in 1998 and the Australian Active Service Medal for his tour of duty to East Timor, in 2001. He was presented with the Iraq Campaign Medal, the Australian Defence Medal and the Iraq Campaign Clasp to the Australian Active Service Medal in 2006. Christopher was also part of a unit citation to the Joint Public Affairs Unit by the Chief of the Defence Force.

For more than thirty years, Christopher (*photo by Robert Hodge*) has been involved in scouting and has run Venturer

Scout Units for boys aged 14 to 18 in both Victoria and NSW. He was instrumental in bringing to life the annual Dragon Skin competition held in New South Wales. Dragon Skin is the largest competition camp held in Australia and  the South Pacific for Venturers and Ranger Guides at Easter, with more than 1200 people participating from Australia and overseas. Christopher was presented the Silver Wattle Award by Scouts Australia in August 2008, for his outstanding service to Scouting.

Christopher holds a Masters degree in Organisational Communication from Charles Sturt University and a Bachelor of Arts degree from the University of Technology, Sydney, where he majored in Journalism and Communications Technology. He is also a Justice of the Peace.

He is married to Yvonne and the couple has three sons. Both Yvonne and Christopher enjoy outdoor recreational activities including camping, abseiling and scuba diving.

"If you can keep your head when all about you are losing theirs and blaming it on you ... you'll be a Man my son!"

If
Rudyard Kipling - 1895

CHAPTER ONE

The Morrow household was in a state of organised turmoil as Scott and the rest of the family rushed to put the finishing touches to their best clothes.

Scott was busy spraying starch on his Scout shirt and ironing it into shape. This was a day he had long looked forward to over the past twelve months. It was a day he knew would be tinged with sadness and also full of happiness when he gathered with the other members of his Venturer unit at Government House.

"Come on Scott or we'll be late!" Scott's mother Kelly called.

"I'm almost finished! Just a few more strokes," Scott replied as he put the finishing touches to his crisply-ironed shirt. "You know I like to have sharp creases in my sleeves."

"Yes, I know, just like Mike's shirts. That man will haunt us for some time," Kelly answered.

Scott, his parents and older brother David, made their way into the family car and drove to the city. Today Scott would be presented with two awards - one for bravery and the other his Queen's Scout Certificate by the State Governor. The Queen's Scout Certificate was the culmination of passing proficiency badges within the teenage section of Scouting called Venturers and was the highest possible award.

The bravery award was something special. It was the highest civilian award that could be handed out by the Government. Scott was nervous and excited.

"Remember, keep a straight back and when the media start talking to you about the bravery award, look the reporters in

1

the eye when answering - not into the camera," Scott's father, Allan cautioned.

"I will. I'll just be glad when today is over so I can go back to living a normal life," Scott said. "I'm tired of the glare of TV cameras. What I did is what anyone else in my circumstances would do."

"Not really. It took guts to take on those clowns and help bring them to justice," David stated as he wound his window down.

The journey to the city took around thirty minutes. The Morrows were indeed lucky today as they were allotted special parking behind Government House. When the Morrows approached the front gate of Government House a media throng was ready to meet them.

"That's him! Roll the cameras! Quickly!" came a yell from a number of news crews waiting to capture Scott and the other award recipients on film.

"Wave to them slowly Scott," Allan told his son.

"Okay."

Allan drove to his designated spot after being guided by State police who were assisting with parking in the grounds.

"I hope he's here. I really do," Scott said to his mum.

"He'll turn up, you watch. Do you really think he would miss your special day?" Kelly said.

"I hope not. It will be good to see him again."

The family alighted from the car and was ushered into the rear entrance of Government House to meet the Governor.

"This place is like a palace. Have a look at the giant chandelier - it must have a million lights in it - never mind the crystal!" Scott was suddenly struck by the grandeur of the main drawing room.

He was introduced to the Governor, a retired Major General who welcomed him with a beaming smile.

"Hello Scott, I have heard so much about you. Welcome to my humble abode," announced General Brian McGrath.

"Humble? This place is fit for a king or queen," Scott replied.

"Well, after all, the house was built with royalty in mind, as this is where they stay if ever the Royal family comes to Sydney."

"Gee, I haven't seen so many stained glass windows and paintings in a house before."

The Governor smiled and said, "If you like, you can come back another time and I'll arrange a personal tour of the house and show you what it is really like."

"That would be cool. Mum, Dad, can I come back and have a look over this palace please?" Scott asked.

"Of course you can. Major General McGrath has invited you, and it would be an honour to see this entire colonial masterpiece," Scott's dad, Allan replied.

Scott mingled with the other guests for around twenty minutes while the grounds of Government House filled to capacity with family members, guests and members of the public. It was a cloudless day with hardly any wind. It was a great day for photos.

The Governor looked out the window and back at his watch and turned to Scott. "Are you ready?"

"Yes," the teenager replied.

"Don't be nervous. You have done your country a great honour and in doing so, helped save the lives of your friends. Be proud of yourself. You deserve it," the General said as he withdrew from the window.

The award recipients moved out of Government House and formed up with the Scout pipe and drum band and marched around the rear gardens to the front gates. The official guests took their seats and the band struck up. The march to the front of Government House with the other Venturers and special award recipients was around 500 metres long.

In Scott's mind it took an eternity. The moment the band master twirled his baton and the band sounded, the crowd started rising to its feet. News crews were at the front of the band filming and then walking beside the marchers. A number of times cameramen walked beside Scott as he proudly marched towards the lawns in front of Government House.

Scott scanned the crowds but he couldn't see Mike, his Venturer leader or any of his fellow Venturers. An air of disappointment started coming over him as he saw the official podium come into view ahead of him. Just then, a pea whistle started sounding and a large banner reading, *Well Done Scott* was hoisted above the crowd.

A chant started rising from somewhere near the banner as the crowd began joining in, "Well done Scott! Well done Scott! Well done Scott!"

The media went berserk and they turned their attention onto the crowd to capture the mood and then back to Scott. Suddenly, a lone Scout lemon-squeezer hat could be seen near the banner and as the crowd started to part to allow the media in, Scott saw his Venturers all turned out in their best uniforms and all singing in unison, "Well done Scott!"

The teenager began to lose it emotionally, until he saw Mike Hunter, his Venturer leader under the lemon-squeezer hat give him a thumbs up. Mike then joined his Venturers in the chorus and the crowd kept the chant going, almost drowning out the band. The bandmaster lifted his baton and the marchers came to a halt.

The band turned left and the marchers went to the right to form a hollow square on the lawns. Scott looked up at Government House and saw the Governor peering down through the curtains at him. When their eyes met, the General closed his fist and also put his thumb up to Scott before allowing the curtains to close again.

The Governor's aide-de-camp came striding out of Government House to the podium. The band stopped playing and Major General McGrath walked out to resounding applause from the now well worked-up crowd. He stood at the podium and the aide-de-camp called the recipients to attention. The band then played the national anthem while the Governor and the recipients saluted. At the end, the Governor called on the recipients to stand easy and for the crowd to sit.

"Distinguished guests, award recipients, ladies and gentlemen. It is not often so much emotion sweeps through these portals, but today is different." Major General McGrath continued. "Today we honour a number of Venturers who have worked hard and tirelessly to obtain the necessary proficiency badges to enable them to receive their Queen's Scout Award - Scouting's highest youth award.

"We also have a number of very special people who have placed self-sacrifice above all the rest and helped their fellow people ..."

The banner from Scott's unit was hoisted high and the Venturers started singing out again, "Well done Scott! Well done Scott!"

The crowd started picking up the chant again and the media suddenly started running back to Scott's Venturers. The Governor paused as he acknowledged the crowd and the chant reached a new crescendo. He waited a few moments and then continued.

"One of our special awardees seems to have captured the hearts of you all, as I know he captured the hearts of our nation recently.

"This is the day we pay special homage to ....."

Scott started to shed a tear as he was overcome with emotion. It had been almost a year since his Venturer unit had gone on their fateful camp. It was the Christmas holidays when the Venturers had ten days together at Myall Lakes near Newcastle on the eastern seaboard of New South Wales.

Scott remembered the trip very well. It was his first ten-day camp away from home, and his first extended camp with Mike and the unit. He had travelled with Mike in his utility along with Steve, his unit chairman. The Unit had been preparing for the holiday camp for months and had done a couple of practice weekend camps too.

Myall Lakes is shaped like a figure of eight, and at its southern boundary it edges onto a narrow sand peninsula that separates it from the ocean. It was an ideal place to camp as the boys could use their surf skis and canoes on the lake or go for a swim in the surf. Situated there was a small camping ground and Mike had pre-booked it twelve months in advance. It was to be the unit's home away from home and palace for the next ten days.

"I can't wait to get the tents up and start canoeing out there," Steve said. "This will be ten days of bliss without Mum and Dad around."

"Yeah, I can't wait either," Scott agreed. "Just think ten glorious days of sleeping in and no alarm clocks going off to get you up ready for school."

"Don't rush into it too fast. Remember you will all be taking turns in organising meals and that means some of you will have to get up well before the others," Mike said.

"Good old Mike," Scott thought. "Trust him to put an organised damper on the activity."

However, he was right. Teams of boys had been organised over the last few weeks so everyone knew their roster for preparing meals, cleaning the dishes and tidying up the campsite. The last thing Mike wanted was a slack unit which would invariably, lead to problems. Mike was a Captain in the Army Reserve and was accustomed to organising personnel. He was a role model the boys and their parents respected. He was gregarious and could mix with both youth and adults on their respective levels as required. The 25 year-old newspaper journalist was worldly and had seen and been involved in things you generally only read about.

Often on camps the boys would ask Mike about his latest stories and how they really unfolded - not just what was reported. It was a great educative process for the boys as they came to realise the difference between what could be legally reported and what actually happened in real life.

Mike told of the murders, deliberately-lit fires and demonstrations he covered for his paper. However, he wasn't one to boast about his knowledge of inside facts. It was the boys who would ask him for more details. Sometimes, Mike would hold back - other times he would let fly if he thought the police or other authorities had deliberately interfered so they wouldn't be reported as being incompetent.

Other Venturers joined Steve and Scott for the camp and had been dropped off by a couple of parents at the bush land camp on the edge of the lakes. One drove a mini bus and the other a sedan so he could take the driver home. The camp itself was nothing spectacular; it was just a clearing near the lakes. Dotted along the foreshore of the lakes were huge pine trees which were great for afternoon shade. Scott was put in charge of erecting the food tent and organising it.

"Grab the barrels and put them over here," he said to Brett and Peter. "I think we should put the water barrel near the front and the other two near the back."

"What about the table and crate?" Peter asked. "The crate will have the fruit in it and needs to be more easily accessible."

"You're right, as usual. We should put the barrels on the sides of the tent and table nearer to the front with the fruit crate on it," Scott replied.

The food containers were large, plastic barrels which had screw-down lids with lists of their contents stuck to the front by tape. One was set aside for fresh water as there were no water pipes nearby.

"What about a tent fly to go over the tent to keep it cooler?" Brett asked.

"As usual, you're right," Scott replied.

"The fly is in the back of Mike's Ute, I'll get it."

Within a short time, the gangly youth had returned with the fly and the three boys quickly erected it over the tent to help provide more shade. While Scott, Peter and Brett worked on the food tent, the others were busy setting up the accommodation tent, mess fly and a latrine area.

"We're only missing one thing now," Mike said to his assembled Venturer unit.

"What's that?" Brett asked.

"The brew point," Mike answered.

"The what?" The chorus went up from the unit.

"Somewhere to get a cup of tea or coffee as required rather than making a fire every time," Mike said.

"Okay, we have one small table left over, maybe we could set up the small stove and a billy on that so we can have a tea or coffee whenever we come out of the water," Scott suggested.

"Okay, let's do it," Mike said.

Within a short time the brew point was erected and the first coffee was poured for Mike.

"Mmm, that's nice. The first brew of the day - I didn't have much time for one this morning," Mike said.

"How's the camp?" Steve asked. "More to the point, what do you all think? Is it easily accessible? Is your gear stowed away and the equipment within reach?"

"Yes and I think it's time we organised lunch," Scott said.

"Good idea. Guys, I think you've done a great job. Well done. Now we have to keep this tidy as the days tick over," Mike cautioned.

The camp was the main event for the year. It was bliss. No parents - just the Venturers and Mike and ten days of adventure on the lakes or in the surf. The camp had taken a couple of hours to pitch and it was time for lunch and the first of a seemingly endless bout of swimming, canoeing and surf skiing. The Venturers revelled with the excitement of doing their own thing. Mike, on the other hand, sat back on a deck chair in the shade of a pine tree. He had a cup of coffee in one hand and a notebook and pen in the other. Scott handed over the surf ski to David, picked up his towel and walked over to Mike.

"What's up? Why aren't you joining in?" he asked.

"I just want to ensure we've thought of everything. You know ... did we bring enough food, spares, first aid – all that sort of thing."

Scott was drying his back when Mike looked up at him and told him to put his sneakers on.

"You know the rules – no sneakers, no swim in the lake," Mike cautioned. "You don't know what people have thrown into the water and if you cut your feet, they may get infected."

"Sorry. I was just so hot after putting up the tents and overhead flys, I forgot."

Scott beamed Mike a smile and Mike smiled back and shook his head. Scott had a large smile that would melt anyone's problems away. Mike always said Scott should join the diplomatic service and help win over hard-nosed adversaries. Scott was different to the other Venturers. He had a smaller frame, near-perfect smooth skin, blonde hair and green eyes that were always enquiring. Scott hadn't gone into Venturers the normal way after progressing from the Scout Troop. He had never been a Scout.

Scott's father Allan was a police officer in the highway patrol and he had initially frowned upon Scott for wanting to join those 'goofy' Venturers. Allan was a macho man, looking to always prove his manhood. His new wife Kelly worked on Allan to help change his attitude. When Scott caught up with some of the caving and abseiling adventures of a couple of his classmates he was spellbound. He got Mike's address and went and saw him unannounced.

Mike had been living in the rear section of a house and was reading a book when he heard the back gate open. He looked up and saw a small, gangly youth open the gate and push his bicycle in and then close the gate behind him. The youth took off his helmet and a shock of blonde hair came into view. The boy was either a young-looking fifteen-year-old or an older thirteen-year-old. Mike followed the boy's progress across the backyard and onto his verandah. The boy knocked on the door and Mike got up to greet him.

"Hello, I'm Scott Morrow, a friend of David and Brett. Are you Mike Hunter?" Scott blurted out.

"Yes and welcome. Come on in."

Mike was instantly taken by the boy's confidence and his aura of geniality. Mike closed the fly screen door and looked at the youth before him. Scott beamed a large smile and suddenly Mike felt totally disarmed.

"David has told me of some of the things you do in Venturers, and I was wondering if I could join please?" Scott asked.

"I hope David wasn't too imaginative in what he told you," Mike said. "Take a seat and I'll go over Venturers with you. Would you like a cup of tea or coffee?"

"No thanks."

"Okay, then let's get straight into it," Mike said.

This first meeting with Scott was etched into Mike's memory banks forever. In one sense there was nothing extraordinary about a boy wanting to join his Venturer Unit; it was just that they normally turned up on Friday nights at the hall with their mates and parents. Instead, here was a slightly-built lad with a smile as big as his head and green eyes fired with determination wanting to join in the fun and games and also start on the path to becoming a Queen's Scout.

Mike knew Scott had been well briefed by David by the way he related his knowledge of Venturers and the things he knew they did. Mike told him about the general activities the unit did and also the various badges he would have to gain to obtain his Queen's Scout Award.

"The nights at the hall and our weekend away will be fun. However, some of the activities you have to undertake to further yourself and test your training could be a little arduous at times," Mike told him.

"What do you mean?" Scott asked.

"Take your expeditions for instance. You have to do two lots of them. The first can be over two days but the second must be over three to four days in unfamiliar country. However, it can be done on foot, bikes, canoes or even a plane."

"A plane?"

"Yep, if you get your pilot's license and organised with your instructor to fly over a challenging route I'm sure it would be approved," Mike said.

Scott was spellbound as Mike described some of the badges and the challenges they brought with them. Time slipped by and Mike checked his watch. "Wow! Sorry for the long burst on Venturers. I got caught up. Now you have some sort of idea, talk to your mum and dad. If they want to ring me then here's my card, otherwise, just come to the hall on any Friday night with them, fill out the registration forms and start straight away. You'll fit right in. If David and Brett are your friends, you won't have a problem."

"Thanks, I really appreciate your help and I look forward to getting involved," Scott said as he stood up.

The audience was over and it was time to go home and tell his mother. She would then help Scott persuade his father to allow him to join. Mike walked Scott to the back gate and watched him ride his bike away.

The boy had been nervous meeting him but seemed to settle down pretty quickly. He was also very keen to start and seemed to have endless questions about some of the activities. In particular abseiling and caving where Mike took the Venturers to a fifteen metre rock face that overlooked the nearby Georges River. The boys never went caving until they could abseil down the cliff face proficiently. Mike didn't want problems with anyone underground when he took them to the caves at Bungonia or Wee Jasper, south of Sydney. He wanted the boys competent enough where he could rely on them to help get him out of problems if he encountered them.

The days and nights on the rock face were spent in teaching mode with various groups being taught by the other Venturers and checked by Mike. Of course abseiling was more than fun – it was an adrenalin rush. A few Venturers that had excelled in their work were taught going over the cliff face first, in what Mike called Forward Geneva. It was a technique similar to one the Army did, only this time there were no weapons slung over shoulders. Mike also taught rescue techniques to the boys and invariably would get them to rescue each other every so often to keep their knowledge current. Caving, on the other hand, was a hoot to the Venturers. They would be dressed in overalls, boots, helmets and gloves most of the weekend.

Abseiling down the pitch-black rock walls and watching the belayer's helmet light grow from less than a pin head in size to full size, was exhilarating. Scrambling over the rocky outcrops, clambering down tight passageways and inching their way up narrow chimneys, or vertical pathways, were an adrenalin rush to many of the boys. Steve had told the story of an overweight Venturer that had gone down one set of caves called the Dragon Teeth. He said the boy was aged around sixteen, but was around fifteen kilos overweight. The unit had abseiled into the cave and over a series of overhanging rocks to reach the cave floor. Slowly they made their way up and over a series of rocky paths in the shape of dragons' teeth.

However, one climb area led the party to a low-slung area with a small ceiling and the overweight Venturer became stuck. The boy's chest was rock hard against the cave ceiling and his breathing started to rapidly increase as he became scared. Mike spoke quietly to a few of the Venturers and they gathered around the stuck boy. Mike calmly spoke to the Venturer and gently stroked his face to ease his apprehension. When the boy relaxed and there was a gap between his chest and the ceiling Mike yelled out and the other three boys pulled their mate clear. The boy broke down and cried with relief, and Mike comforted him until the youth could calm himself. The Venturers then continued on their way through the tricky cave until they found the final shaft leading out.

Scott thought all his wishes had come true when his dad said he could join Venturers. Allan wanted to meet with this Mike and check him out. Scott pondered that for a second. His dad wanted to see what sort of man Mike was. This would be interesting. The highway patrolman meets the Army Reserve Captain and journalist. Friday couldn't come fast enough. However, the meeting proved to be a non-event. Allan had worn his uniform deliberately to try and intimidate Mike. The tables quickly turned when Mike shook hands with him and welcomed him to the hall.

Mike made a point to ask whether Allan knew Superintendent Ralph Sorenson, the State Head of the Highway Patrol.

"Yes," the policeman answered. Mike replied he would be having lunch with him next week in relation to a story he was working on and would pass on his compliments. Allan smiled, filled out Scott's registration forms and left. Scott looked inquisitively at Mike but he just smiled, gave him the thumbs up and laughed. That was it – Scott was in. He had only to be invested and he would be a fully-fledged Venturer.

CHAPTER TWO

The day had been full of activity and the night was shaping up to be no better. No sooner had the sun started going down and tea for the Venturers was starting to be cooked. Scott was in charge of the first night's tea - spaghetti bolognaise, tinned fruits and custard. Mike had told the boys how to prepare the meal and now it was up to them. Scott considered himself lucky. By preparing the meal he didn't have to wash or wipe up the plates. It didn't take the newcomer long to organise the mince to be cooked, onions to be cut and sautéed and the spaghetti boiled. He added the obligatory cans of crushed tomatoes and tomato soup and was excited when he tasted it to find the meal was scrumptious. Phew! The last thing Scott wanted was the reputation of not being able to cook a simple meal.

After dinner and when the trestle tables were cleared, Mike sat down with the Venturers and had a planning session with them. He wanted to make sure they were organised for activities, timings, transport and work rosters.

'Geez,' Scott thought. 'If Venturers is like this and this is only a simple camp, what would it be like for an army unit? Would Mike go through so much detail? Probably.'

Scott had fallen in love with the lifestyle of the Venturers. Instead of moping around the house or maybe going on a bike ride with some of his friends looking for something to do, he could achieve something for himself in the Venturers. He could learn about bush craft, knots, abseiling, caving, first aid and anything else he wanted to find out about. The interesting thing about these Venturers is that Mike never really ran the unit or its meetings. Scott had heard about Scouts and how their meetings were organised mostly by their leaders. Here it was different. The boys had the chance to choose their own pathways and take on the training required for the activity through Mike or other leaders outside the unit.

The smell of the pines and the gentle lapping of the water on the edge of the lakes were constantly in the background as the Venturers went about their activities. Sometimes, when the wind picked up, it would whistle through the trees producing an eerie noise.

"So it's decided then. Tomorrow we'll hit the lake first thing and do some canoeing around its edges to see what's there. After lunch when it's hotter, we'll go to the surf," Mike stated.

The Venturers agreed.

"When do you want to explore the old submarine?" Steve asked.

"That's up to you," Mike replied. "I'd say get used to these surroundings first, and when you are bored with them then let's go further afield. Probably in a few days, I'd suggest."

"Sounds good to me."

"How far is the sub out from the shore?" Brett asked.

"Not far. About a kilometre."

"Tell us again Mike how the sub got there," David piped up.

"Steve, it's your turn," Mike said as he handed over the question to the unit chairman.

"It was being towed to Japan after being decommissioned. My understanding is, the boat was to be made into scrap and come back here as razor blades and other metal products."

"That's fine, but how did it end up on shore here?" Brett queried.

"During the towing operation, a large storm hit and the sub broke free of its tow lines and grounded on rocks just north of here," Steve replied.

He had been told the story by Mike before who had also shown Steve the newspaper clippings of the event.

"The government decided the sub could stay as a sort of tourist attraction. Problem is, you can only get to it at very low tide and a long swim or with snorkelling or diving equipment."

Scott's mind was racing. Here was a genuine Navy submarine and the boys had all the time in the world to explore it during the holidays. What an adventure!

"Can you get into the sub and go through all its holds?" Scott asked.

"No. The Navy apparently sealed the hatches shut. However, you never know, we might find a way in," Steve answered.

"Yeah, us and a million others," lamented David. "If the sub's hatches were open, water would get in and the sub would rust from the inside out and cause a major pollution problem. My bet is, the Navy welded shut the hatches."

"I don't care," Scott said. "Just swimming out to it and exploring it is a tremendous thing for me and I'm looking forward to it."

"Well done Scott. Regardless of whether the hatches are welded shut or not, the adventure of swimming out to a submarine and exploring it should be fantastic," Mike said.

"Brett, we'll have to take a couple of the surf skis with us as a backup," Steve suggested.

"Good planning maestro," Brett replied.

No naked flames were allowed in the campsite area. This was a bit of a let-down for the boys, as they loved sitting around a campfire, telling jokes, listening to some stories from Mike or just taking in the warm glow of the flames and embers. Myall Lakes at Christmas time is a hot, dry area and any flame could easily have started a major bushfire along the lake's shores. Instead, the boys used their time sitting around the trestle table and playing games, listening to their music and talking. Scott walked to the edge of the lake and grabbed hold of the overhanging branch of a pine tree and stared into nothingness across the placid waters. He was taken by the beauty of the place. The campsite was a long way from the nearest town and there were no main lights from industry or any built-up areas that could be seen.

"It's as if God threw a huge handful of diamonds into the air and they froze in time," Mike said as he stood next to Scott to take in the view.

"I've never seen so many stars before. Are there always this many?"

"Yes," answered Mike. "This show is on nightly. It's just that back home we have so many lights in our suburbs and cities that we can't always see all the stars."

"I've been camping with Mum and Dad before but still I haven't seen so many stars," Scott said without shifting his gaze.

"Scott, as long you can gain some enjoyment from these natural wonders, you'll really enjoy life. The water tickling the side of the lake when the breeze flows through and the singing of the trees as they wave their branches, are beautiful experiences," Mike extolled.

Scott looked at Mike. "You know I'm pretty thankful for being here. This is one experience I didn't want to miss," he said.

"Hopefully this and every other Venturer activity will be things you won't want to miss. For now, think about tomorrow and how much sleep you need."

"You're right. I'm feeling pretty stuffed. I just want to take in the sight a bit longer, and then I'll go to bed," Scott said as he flashed one of his disarming smiles.

"Okay, enjoy it and good night," Mike said.

"Good night Mike."

Mike made his way back to the main mess fly and tables to where the rest of the boys who were still up were playing cards. Scott looked across the lake and saw the reflection of the moon cast across the water. It was surrounded in the sky by millions of bright diamond-like grains of sand. The picture was mesmerising and comforting. It was a giant show of nature and Scott was the only one watching it.

"Thank you God .... it's great," Scott murmured as he turned his head from the heavens and went to his tent for his first night's sleep on the camp.

CHAPTER THREE

Vitali had been waiting all day for the phone to ring. He paced his Sydney apartment drinking his thick Russian coffee. Finally the silence was pierced by the high-pitched ring of his mobile phone.

"We have arrived," the voice on the other end said in fluent Russian.

"What took so long?" an anxious Vitali asked.

"Delays at Kennedy International and our transfers to Sydney. We'll be with you within the hour."

The phone went dead and a relieved Vitali threw the device on the table. 'At last,' he thought, 'it starts.' Vitali was the front man for a Russian mafia group who were about to pull off one of their most daring drug operations Down Under. The group had chosen Australia because of its vast, virtually unpatrolled coastline and burgeoning drug trade. Vitali was fluent in English as he had gone to Cambridge University to study history. This study also allowed him to build up a repertoire of necessary skills and contacts before embarking on the plunge Down Under. Before leaving Moscow, Vitali was a small-time criminal who loved to live the high life. One day he crossed paths with the criminal elite when a protection racket he was trying to set up went wrong. Unbeknown to Vitali, the Russian mafia was also trying to extort money from the same department store as he was. He was caught in his own sting at gunpoint and taken before the head mafia boss and questioned at length.

Vitali was a fast talker and he managed to convince the mafia dons to let him join forces with them and so, stay alive. The price was high. Vitali was ordered to front a major operation in Australia and set up a flow-line for future drug imports. If he set things in motion the right way, he earned his life, if not? Well, Vitali did not want to think along those lines. He could see many benefits for himself, including staying alive. The hour went quickly now as Vitali checked his equipment and went over his plans in his head. The knock at the door broke the quiet. Vitali checked through the eye-viewer and recognised the two faces looking back at him. He quickly unlatched the door.

"Good to see you brother," Vitali said as he gave the biggest man a bear hug. "You also cousin."

Vitali gave the second man a hug too and motioned for them both to enter his apartment.

"Vitali, Rudi sends his greetings and hopes all is in train," Dimitri said. His moustache twitched and Vitali wanted to laugh but held back and kept a serious face.

"Yes, yes, all is well. The ship arrives in two days time and will drop off the cargo for us to pick up," Vitali assured the men.

"Good, good."

Dimitri nodded to the second man, Boris, who asked, "Have you got our dive gear and transport organised?"

"Yes, I hope I have the right sizes for you." Vitali was feeling good about his organisational skills. "We have plenty of time to go over our plans. Let's organise some food and wine first," he suggested.

"Excellent. That plane food on the ... what do you call it? Skippy airlines? It tasted like plastic," Boris complained.

The three men laughed and adjourned to the kitchen to organise some food.

CHAPTER FOUR

"Are you sure the sub is still there?" Brett asked Mike over a morning coffee.

"Well, we can check it out this afternoon when we go to the lighthouse. It should be visible just north of it," Mike answered.

"What about the lighthouse? Can we get inside and have a look around - that would be cool?" Brett said as he sipped his golden brew.

"The lighthouse has been closed for a number of years but I think National Parks now operate tours of the place," Mike offered. "I haven't been here for years so I'm not really sure."

He looked to where all the noise was coming from and started laughing. The Venturers had put their cricket stumps into the lake and were playing water cricket with a tennis ball. The batsman hit the ball and the fielders were able to take large dives for it and land in the water and create a huge splash.

"Get a load of the dolphins out there, will you," Mike said to Brett as the two of them followed the antics of Steve and the others.

"Well, that's it, I'm in!" Brett took off his T-shirt and ran to the water, performing a 360-degree somersault when he hit the deep parts.

Mike sat back and watched the Venturers play. This was camaraderie at its best. The boys didn't have a care in the world and they were mixing in really well, so far. The test would come around day four or five when the Venturers had more than settled into a routine and they became bored with their surroundings. Mike knew they had to be kept busy with activities and challenges to keep their spirits up and also stop any boredom.

The water cricket was a hit. Mike had to stop the game only once to get the boys to either wear their sun protective rash shirts to stop sunburn or have the boys apply sunscreen to each other. Frolicking in the water was the order of the day for each of the days of camp. Other campers had descended onto the main camping area in droves and set up a virtual tent city about one hundred metres from the Venturers. Just like home, the campers would put their rubbish out every few days and unlike home, a Council truck would drive through the campsite. A couple of men would run beside the truck, pick up the rubbish and throw it up to another man who would place it on the truck. A piece of cake! It came time for the boys' latrine to be disposed of. They had erected a small hessian tent with a toilet seat on a small stand which opened onto a garbage bag – simple. When the bag was full, it was tied off and then disposed of.

Mike was struggling to think of where to empty the bag when Brett suggested it should be put with the campers' rubbish. It would be disposed of by the garbage men with no problems. Mike was apprehensive. Mark, one of the Venturers, donned a large pair of ski goggles, a beanie and tied a tea towel around his face like a political demonstrator. He then put on a pair of abseiling gloves and went to the latrine and tied off the bag and replaced it with a fresh one. Mark then quietly took the bag and put it among the campers' bags and stealthily made his way back to camp. It was early morning and the garbage truck was due within the hour. The boys set up their water cricket and started playing.

"Here she comes!" Scott yelled.

"Ssshhh!" warned Steve. "Keep playing."

The truck wound its way through the camp with the two men picking up the garbage bags and throwing them onto the truck. The Venturers kept watching and playing simultaneously. The truck stopped outside the main group of bags and Mark sat down in the water. He could see it coming! The first few bags were hoisted easily to the man on the top and then thrown into some sort of order around the tray of the truck. Then the smaller garbage man picked up the Venturers' bag, struggled a bit with it, and tried to throw it to the top of the truck. Splat! The bag was too heavy for the man to throw properly and it hit the sides of the truck and started falling. The man fumbled under it and the bag split and its contents splashed onto the truck and ground. The Venturers burst into riotous laughter and started ducking under the water so they couldn't be heard. The poor garbage man was hitting the sides of the truck and kicking the tyres while his two workmates were doubled over with laughter. Within a couple of minutes the garbage men cleaned off the truck with water from a jerry can and poured sand on the mess on the ground in an attempt to try and solidify what they could. After the clean-up, the man who had been hit with the Venturers' waste climbed to the top of the truck and the other two went into the cabin before it drove off. The Venturers continued their cricket while the truck drove off and then they started again in fits of laughter.

"That's it boys. No more of that. From now on we'll find the toilets in town to empty the latrine into," Mike said.

"Your little incident could have caused that man any sort of grief with sickness if he's not inoculated."

"But did you see it?" Brett asked. "What a shit throw!"

"What a shit catch!" chorused Mark, as the Venturers again doubled up with laughter.

"Come on guys let's have a brew and work out this afternoon's activity," Mike said, changing the subject.

The Venturers pulled up the stumps and went to the shore to dry off and get their coffee mugs. Mike usually put a billy of water on around 10 a.m. for 'mornos' or morning tea. The boys organised their fresh water, cordial and tea and coffee. They grabbed some fruit and biscuits and sat down.

"Get some canoeing in within the next two hours then we'll head up to the Seal Rocks lighthouse," Mike said. "It's a great place to view any whales that may pass and the whole place is steeped in history."

"Like what?" David asked.

"Well, it was built by convicts last century to aid shipping as it plied northwards to round Queensland and head home to England."

"So what's so interesting about that?" Scott queried.

"Well, this lighthouse is different. It was built at a time when the Colony had mobile prisons – sort of paddy wagons drawn by horses. These wagons would take the convicts to different farms and Government jobs and overseers would ensure the convicts worked to fulfill the job.

"Problem was the Governor at the time kept getting reports from ships warning of dangerous outcrops of rocks near Seal Rocks. Also, there were a number of graziers who had settled in the district and the Governor said he would help them by building some bridges and roads in the area," Mike said.

"So what makes the lighthouse different?" Scott repeated, not wanting his question to be lost.

"Thanks Scott, I get caught up in detail and sometimes forget the question at hand," Mike looked at his young charge.

"There weren't enough mobile prison vans for the convicts so the Governor decided to build a small prison at Seal Rocks and the lighthouse came later.

"It's a fascinating place, considering all the rock was cut by hand at a nearby quarry and carried into the area on horse-drawn vehicles."

"This could be a great place to play war games," Scott suggested as he thought of the water pistol he had brought but hadn't used yet.

"Could be," agreed Steve. "We'll have to check it out first, to make sure we don't have any problems. Bring your water pistols just in case."

Mike motioned with his hands for the Venturers to stay put for a moment. "There's one other good thing about this place. The lighthouse and prison annex were built virtually on the edge of the cliff line. Who knows? It could make a great place to abseil. We'll have to check that out too."

One of the games the Venturers loved was war games, where they would divide into two groups and stalk each other to recover some great prize, usually a flashing light or something similar. They liked playing at Oatley Park near their hall where a large picnic area had been built in the shape of a medieval castle during the Great Depression to help provide work for the locals. The park was situated at the end of a peninsula and surrounded either side by the Georges River. The other favourite spot for the Venturers was at La Perouse on the northern headland of Botany Bay, just south of Sydney. During the Second World War, the Australian Army built a series of bunkers there and placed a number of artillery guns to help repel any invaders. The bunkers were abandoned after the war and eventually the National Parks department took control of the area as part of public lands. The boys loved the area because no one else was there after nightfall and the place was theirs to use. It was a great place to run and hide among the myriad of rooms within the bunkers or search for the flashing light. It was also a good place to catch someone unawares with a water pistol as they walked or 'patrolled' near you. The water pistols the

Venturers used weren't the little handheld types used by small children, but huge two-handed types, some connected to a backpack of water, and all capable of delivering a good dousing.

CHAPTER FIVE

Dimitri made the first shore-to-ship call five hours after arriving at Vitali's apartment. The plan was simple. A small boat would be lowered from the side of a container ship as it steamed south towards Sydney. The small boat would make its way to Seal Rocks just before dawn and two divers would drop off the packages of heroin on the submarine. By doing it this way, the packages were quite safe from holiday-makers, as the tide would be high and the boat could slip in and out of Seal Rocks without being seen. Sometime later, Vitali and his crew were to pick up the white powder of addiction and take it to Sydney – ready to be distributed.

"Everything is set. The Pushkin will be off Seal Rocks on Wednesday morning," Dimitri announced.

"Vitali, is our accommodation booked?"

"Yes. I have three separate rooms booked in the motel. However, you need to try on your wetsuits and ensure they fit you okay," Vitali suggested.

"Fine, fine. Get the wetsuits and we'll try them on now."

The three Russians spent the rest of the day checking out their equipment and going over their plans. Vitali had organised a number of drug wholesalers to meet with them on the Thursday. These drug distributors had their own networks around Sydney's beaches, the city's sex-trade area of Kings Cross and among the communities of Cabramatta, in Sydney's west.

In another part of Sydney, Customs Officers stood shoulder to shoulder in the briefing room. This was the first time overtime had been relaxed for some months. The briefing could only mean something extraordinary was about to occur. Among the sky-blue coloured shirts, was a sprinkling of soldiers in their familiar peanut-butter coloured camouflage uniforms. Also present were a number of civilians, some with pretty unkempt hair.

"Okay, I can understand maybe why the soldiers are here," Customs Officer Jim Brown said to his partner, Dave Cosgrove.

"We have worked with them before. But who the hell are the civvies?"

"Easy. They are members of the SASR - the Special Air Service Regiment. Some are counter-terrorist experts, the others are Federal police." Dave replied.

"This should be interesting. They catch the baddies and we read them the Customs regulations before the Feds take them into custody. Phew!"

The crowd parted as the head Customs officer made his way through the assembled throng. Superintendent Clive Hartcher had been in Customs for twenty-five years. The career public servant had participated in many sting operations. Now, he was helping direct a multi-agency sting with international links.

"Today is the beginning of the end of Operation Stella," Supt Hartcher announced. "We have tracked the Russian mafia operatives from Moscow to Sydney - thanks to our friends in the Russian secret service and a host of special agents and operatives. Now we have to corner our quarry and lead them to where we want them."

The briefing was interrupted by an officer who took a mobile phone call. "The 'tsars' have arrived. The Pushkin is two days from the coast."

A huge smile came over Supt Hartcher's face. A scruffy civilian and an army colonel put their hands on his shoulder and broke into quiet conversation with him. Within a few moments Supt Hartcher raised his hand and asked for quiet.

"Inspector Julia Lee from Customs House will give the formal brief."

"Listen up. Situation. The situation is ...."

CHAPTER SIX

Mike and the Venturers decided to cool off with a game of water cricket. Greg had emptied a plastic barrel of gear and took it about waist-high into the lake. There he half-filled it with water and replaced the lid. It was now the stumps. Steve used a canoe paddle as the bat, while Peter used a tennis ball as the game's ball. The Venturers were only wearing costumes or board shorts and lashings of sunburn cream. This was Christmas and it was bloody hot! Campers along the lake stopped in awe as the Venturers bowled, batted and tried to catch the ball using water gymnastics.

The bowler would try and run in the waist-high water and then bowl at the water barrel. The fielders took great delight in leaping for the ball, whether it was in range or not - just for the sake of being able to crash back into the cool water like breaching whales. The aerobatics kept the other campers quite amused for some time. Water cricket hadn't been seen on the lake before. If there was one thing the Venturers would be remembered for, it was the active fun they showed in their water cricket games. Scott absolutely reveled in water cricket. It gave him the chance to play with an extended family of brothers - ones that took the time to play with him and teach him to throw, catch, leap and fall into the water with great effect. Mike played fieldsman so the boys could excel and have a ball without some adult overshadowing them. He watched the boys at play and took note of how each interacted. Mike knew some may get homesick, while others would shine. Others like Scott seemed to be on a high from all the bonding.

Mike noted this and knew the hardest time for Venturers like Scott was the week after they returned home when they were away from the close bonds of being with the other boys. For some it was a slow comedown while for others with a couple of brothers, it was no problem at all. Scott was on a constant high. In camp he seemed to have a regular supply of 'brothers'. In the tents were groups of boys. Sitting at the meal tables were groups of boys. Virtually everywhere Scott turned there were always Venturers.

In one sense, this was what Venturing was all about - communing with others and together, helping each other to learn and share experiences. Scott was in his element. He looked forward to each day with relish. Every sunrise brought a new adventure. Scott felt quite content and at home - regardless of the flies and heat by day and the mosquitoes and humidity at night. The constant throng of Venturers going about their normal lives made camp life like ordinary family life. Yes, there were a few arguments, but usually the older boys helped broker peace. Rarely did Mike have to step in. He believed in self-management and teamwork. This meant the team owned the problem and it was up to the team to solve it as one.

This process took a little getting used to, but it worked. Mike also had a secondary process in play. He teamed older Venturers with younger ones. This was not to allow the younger ones to be led astray, but for the older ones to act as mentors. Brett was Scott's mentor. They were complete opposites, even in looks. Scott had blonde hair that was slightly wavy and green eyes. Brett had straight, dark brown hair that bordered on black. He also had brown eyes. Whereas Brett was tall and athletic-looking with large, strong hands; Scott was slight with a medium build and medium to small size hands.

What Scott lacked in physical stature, he made up for in determination. Brett was the atypical soldier within the unit who would look right at home in an army unit. Scott, on the other hand, was more placid and gentle with a strong love for young children. He was gentle but not effeminate. The last of the players was caught out with a magnificent catch from mid-on by David. Steve had sliced at the ball and David had thrust his two hands out in front of him as he leapt high into the air. His fingers grasped the ball hard and he erupted with a deafening yell of, "Howzat!" Steve had no choice but bow out gracefully.

"It's high time you all put more sunscreen on and drank some good water," Mike advised the boys. "The last thing I need now is someone going down with sunstroke or a bad case of sunburn. Peter, organise some cordial so we can replace some of those litres of sweat you all poured into the lake."

"Okay Mike. Mark, give me a hand please? Go into the stores tent and get the cordial. Ian, you can organise the cups and Stuart, you can organise some biscuits, please."

Peter was a strong organiser and would easily have been at home as a sergeant in the army. Mike was not intentionally trying to build a platoon of future soldiers. In fact, he rarely spoke to the boys of his military exploits unless asked. He had made the choice to join the Army Reserve and it was up to the boys to make their own lifestyle choices. Mike saw himself more as a role model for someone who loved the outdoors and the adventure it brought. He also loved the challenge of taking the boys abseiling and helping them overcome their fear of heights and turning it into a positive force to overcome other challenges. Eventually, the Venturers would learn to harness this feeling of overcoming fear and using it to fight other fears, such as going for job interviews. This was an emotional tie to Mike the Venturers would not know they had until they had to call on their inner self to master situations in the future.

Mike had built himself a legacy and he never knew it. If he had known, he would have stopped participating in Venturers, as Mike was never in it for himself, but to further the teenagers in his care. Mike had the Army Reserve to prove himself as an adult among his own peers, not young teenagers. The fingers of darkness started stretching across the lake. All along the figure of eight shoreline lanterns could be seen being lit. Peter organised for a couple of lanterns to be placed along the main trestle tables so Ian and Steve could start preparing the main meal. Ordinarily the meal would have been cooked in daylight and eaten between twilight and dark.

However, the Venturers were exhausted from their water cricket escapades. Mike knew the Venturers would be tired from being out on the sun all day, plus being so active with their water cricket. The very thought of the boys' water follies brought a smile to his face.

"So what's on the menu tonight?" Scott asked Peter.

"Check out the front of the food barrels," Peter replied.

"There's a menu list there along with what is needed to cook the meals each night."

"That's pretty clever," Scott said.

"Get used to it, for when it is your turn to cook you'll need to know what's where."

Scott beamed one of his huge smiles. Peter returned the smile and shook his head. He looked at Mike who nodded in silent agreement. Both had seen new, young Venturers ready to get into their first jobs in camp. Then, when they must perform in front of their peers, they often found excuses to not go to camp.

"What? What's wrong?" Scott asked as he looked at both Mike and Peter.

"Nothing," Mike answered. "Are you ready for tea? Got your mess kit organized? Come on Scott, get your act together." Mike patted Scott on the head. "Go and get your things."

The nightly meal for the Venturers wasn't quite like home. There was no grace said, no father or mother at the head of the table. Mike, as the only adult, sat anywhere. His rules were simple: wash your hands before tea, cleanup after yourself and work as a team to prepare the meal and wash and wipe up afterwards. Mike would not allow the Venturers the luxury of not doing the dishes after each meal. He didn't want any health or hygiene problems if he could help it. He had the Venturers draw up rosters for each of their respective tasks so everyone knew who was expected to do what, and when. The rosters worked and brought about a form of discipline, enforced by the teams and the Venturers themselves. The boys had rigged a dining fly as one of their first tasks in camp. This gave them somewhere to shelter out of the sun and rain. They also erected two trestle tables. The boys had to supply their own fold-up seats or stand during meals. They all brought chairs. The tables were great for preparing meals, washing up afterwards and for playing games on. Scott and the others were pretty tired after being in the hot sun all day playing water cricket. Tonight would be an early to bed night maybe, depending on what games were played on the tables. Sometimes a series of games would be played in tandem as you couldn't fit fifteen boys around most board games. After tea, as the last of the washing up was being put away Steve got Mike's attention.

"Okay Mike let's plan our attack on the sub."

"Alright, gather everyone here for a brief in five minutes," Mike said. "This will give me time to get my maps out."

Steve called a few of the boys together and told them to spread the word about the meeting. Brett ensured the mosquito-repellent candles were lit and placed around the table again. They had been used for tea and some had been put away. It didn't take long for the boys to assemble. Mike unrolled a military-style map of the area where the submarine lay and the nearby lighthouse.

"You all know about the sub's history, so I won't bore you with that," Mike said. "However, I just want to go over a few things about our swim around the sub. Firstly, the sub could be few hundred metres off shore or only one hundred metres off shore. It depends on the tides at this time of year. Either way, we are in for long swim there and back. Do you think you can all make it?"

"If it is so far out why didn't it sink?" Ian asked.

"It foundered on rocks, which is why the government decided to leave it," Mike replied.

"But it's a bit far for tourists to see unless they have a boat," Mark chipped in.

"I thought it was left there mainly for the fish," Scott added.

Mike took control again. "The sub was left in place as a marine habitat and also so divers could explore it.

"Ordinarily, I wouldn't take you out there unless it was by boat. However, as most of you have body boards, we should manage alright as long as we stick together and follow some basic rules ..."

The boys listened intently as Mike went over his plans. The way he outlined the event with back-up details was almost out of a military manual. Mike was not a parent, but was the closest to one for these boys during camp and he wanted no mishaps. He didn't mind introducing the Venturers to the dangers of abseiling, caving and basic rock climbing, but all these had back-up safety aspects.

His main concern was losing one of the boys to an asthma attack or something similar. Thoughts of boys floating unconscious in the water swept over Mike and were quickly dismissed. He knew his Venturers and he had only strong, positive thoughts of the boys and their prowess. The boys were up early the next day. Peter ensured the duty patrol had cleaned up well and all Venturers had secured their tents.

Mark made sure a barrel of fresh water was placed in the rear of the mini bus. Ian organised for sandwiches to be made and a heap of fruit to be included. Steve organised the cordial and a small gas stove and billy for those who wanted a cup of tea or coffee afterwards.

"Don't forget the first aid kit and tell everyone to bring or wear their rash shirts or a T-shirt they can swim in," Peter told Steve.

Mike nodded and added, "Brett, ensure the maps and compasses are loaded."

"Okay boss!" Brett scurried away to retrieve the gear.

Scott was excited. He had never seen a submarine close up before, never mind clamber all over it. His dad had bought him a one-use waterproof camera so he could use it when snorkelling. He could just imagine photos of himself at the conning tower or on top of the sub. His dad would be proud. Body boarding took on a whole new meaning when you actually used the foam boards to take you somewhere with purpose.

"Hey Brett, do you think we'll be able to get inside the sub?" Scott asked.

"I wouldn't think so. I imagine the Navy welded her shut before she was to be towed to Japan for scrap," Brett replied. "But then again, now she has been wrecked she could have opened up when she hit the rocks."

A huge smile suddenly raced across Scott's face.

"Don't even think of going inside," Brett said. "You heard Mike last night. There may be small gashes on the side that would let us in. However, we don't know what marine animal may have taken up residence inside."

Scott pondered for a moment. "I guess if we went inside without scuba gear we could get trapped. I can just imagine all of us inside one of the compartments and our weight tilting the sub off the rocks to the bottom. Phew, not a pleasant thought."

Mike helped stow the body boards and other gear in the trailer behind the mini bus. He did a double-check with Peter and Steve to ensure everything was in order.

"Okay, let's load up and head to our sub," Mike announced. "This should be a top adventure for us all."

Scott felt the camera in his pocket. He winked at Brett and made his way onto the bus. The others followed suit. Peter and Mike took the front passenger and driver seats. Mike adjusted his seat belt and looked around in the cabin. The sight brought a smile to his face. He could see a sea of fluorescent-painted noses, brightly-coloured hats and rash shirts. The scene resembled something out of the Muppets. The weather was good with a cloudless sky, light breeze and low humidity - for the moment. The summer sun was yet to make its real presence felt.

Scott loved this sort of adventure, as it was low-cost and something he could enjoy with everyone. It was also something most of his classmates would never undertake - it may take them out of their comfort zones. Scott nodded to himself. This is the life for him - adventure, with a twist.

CHAPTER SEVEN

Vitali checked the dive gear. The wetsuits fitted the three men perfectly and they were all well-practiced in diving. Dimitri packed the gear into the rear of their four-wheel drive parked in the hotel basement. All was now ready. Vitali made a telephone call to his contact in Cabramatta.

"Gus, this is Leo. We're all set for the pickup."

"When will I see you?" Gus asked.

"If all goes well, the day after tomorrow. I'll ring you when I'm on the way to the Lotus Room."

"Okay. Don't stuff up, as I have some big fish to feed," came the reply.

"No probs. See you soon." Vitali replaced the receiver. It was time to go and scout the location.

Tucked away in Sydney near the harbour waterfront was the Royal Australian Navy's Maritime Headquarters. Deep within the bowels of the building was a large room full of wall-mounted computer screens. This was part of the Operations area that tracked shipping around the globe. It also monitored shipping in Australian waters. Commander Christian O'Shea downloaded the latest satellite imagery of ships heading north from Sydney. He turned to his Warrant Officer.

"Paul you'd better take these to the old man. The Pushkin is right on time."

"Aye sir Coastwatch has been told not to use obvious surveillance," Warrant Officer Smith cautioned.

"Thanks Paul."

Warrant Officer Smith left the room with a collection of photos in a red folder. Across town at Circular Quay, Customs House was also buzzing with activity. Superintendent Hartcher called Inspector Troy Owens to his office.

"Troy, what is the latest with the Pushkin?"

The younger man came into the office with a satellite map of the New South Wales coast. He placed it on his boss's desk and then produced a plastic overlay of the map showing the Pushkin's route.

"At 1100 hours today, the Pushkin was fifty nautical miles south of Seal Rocks," Inspector Owens reported. "At their rate of knots, we expect the ship to be near Taree by tomorrow nightfall. So, now for the million-dollar question: where do you think they'll drop their precious cargo?"

Troy looked his boss square in the eye and said there were hundreds of coves along that part of the coast where a ship could weigh anchor and send a rubber ducky to shore.

"That's not the answer I was hoping to hear," Superintendent Hartcher said. "We'll have to keep a very close watch on her in case she gets spooked and heads out of our waters."

"No probs boss. I'm in constant touch with Navy Operations. Any change, and you'll be the first to know."

"Thanks Troy."

In a cream, multi-storey building at the back of Darlinghurst, just outside of the Sydney CBD, the lights of the Australian Federal police headquarters were burning brightly.

"Matt, are you there?" Inspector Dave Farrell asked as leant across his desk.

"Yes boss," Senior Sergeant Matt Rose replied.

"Matt come in for a minute so I can update you on the Russian mafia boys," Inspector Farrell said.

The junior officer took a seat in his boss's office. The walls were filled with degrees and diplomas from universities and police colleges internationally. Matt poised his pen on his notebook ready to take notes. "Navy Ops has just told me the Pushkin is still two days away from any port large enough to berth her."

"I guess that will be somewhere near Taree then, sir?"

"Yes, that's right. Do we still have our own tail on the Pushkin?"

"Sir, we have two teams leapfrogging positions to try and keep her in sight off the coast. We are also receiving regular updates from the Navy and Coastwatch. The moment the ship gets any closer to shore we'll be onto them. We can then get the local boys involved quickly."

"Sir, there is one thing," Sergeant Rose added.

"Yes?"

"How long will the SASR remain on standby?"

"As long as necessary or until another priority job comes along," Inspector Owens said.

"Thanks sir. Let's hope they're not needed at all," Sergeant Rose added.

CHAPTER EIGHT

Scott could hardly wait to ride his board out to the sub. Excitement had been mounting inside him all night.

"You know, I actually dreamt last night I was the Captain of the sub and I took it for a sail with all our Venturers onboard," Scott said quietly to Brett.

"Did we go far, or just out to sea?" Brett asked as he smiled at Scott.

"I guess it was pretty far as we were gone all day," Scott replied.

The two boys laughed as they joked about who would be second-in-command and they imagined what sort of adventures they could get up to.

"Just imagine we took the sub out to sea and some kind of naval exercise was going on," Scott said excitedly.

"We could slip between the ships playing the blue and orange forces and cause absolute havoc. Both sides wouldn't know who we were!"

Brett grinned. "If both sides didn't know who we were and they both fired on us we'd have a hard time escaping."

Scott looked at Brett and started laughing. "You're right you know. We'd probably be cornered and blasted out of the water before we could surface and hoist our Venturer unit flag. Then again, imagine the looks on the crews when we came on deck in Scout uniform!"

Brett ruffled Scott's hair and told him to go on dreaming, as it was good for him. The noise level in the mini-bus was higher than normal and Mike knew the boys were excited about the adventure before them. He did a mental check of what he had brought with him.

Peter picked up on Mike's vibes. "Water, cordial, lunches, first aid kits ... they're all packed," Peter turned to Mike.

"I can read you like a book now."

"Well after three years in the unit, I'd expect so," Mike replied.

"We've been through a lot of experiences together. Everything from your first bushwalk with the unit, to your first abseil down a fifty metre rock face in a cave."

"It's been great Mike and we have a great bunch of kids in the unit now," Peter said. "In one sense, it will be sad to leave the unit after I turn eighteen – however, I'm looking forward to the challenges of being a Rover and going for my gold Duke of Edinburgh award. That will suffice me."

Mike flashed a smile at Peter. "If you were in the army, I'd serve with you anywhere Pete."

The ginger-haired unit chairman was taken aback. Mike saw him flummoxed and helped out. "In the services, what I just said is considered a compliment. It means you are a top soldier who commands respect by his actions, not just words."

"Thanks Mike. I appreciate that. I have tried hard to not just be one of the boys, but someone they could look up to – like you."

"If you keep this up, I'll start getting emotional," Mike said as he took a firmer grip on the steering wheel.

"Are we there yet Dad?" Ian yelled out from the middle of the bus.

"No, not yet Ian!" rang out a chorus from within the bus. Ian had mimicked a television commercial about a child constantly asking his parents when they would arrive at their destination.

Mike and the senior boys had decided to drive to a headland that overlooked the cove where the submarine lay half-submerged. This way, they could check the water conditions and see whether there were any hazards between the beach and the boat. Mike used his binoculars to scan the cove and the sub. He was not feeling good.

"Guys, I think we have a few problems we need to solve collectively. Each of you, have a look through these at the sub and the stretch of beach leading to it."

Steve was first to have a look. "It's okay to me. What's the problem Mike?"

"Let's all have a look first, and then discuss it as a group," Mike replied.

One by one the boys took hold of the field glasses and scanned the waterway and boat. The surf was running high with most waves breaking away from the beach. On two fronts, waves seemed to break across the beach and not directly onto it. The sub had small waves crashing into it almost along its entire tube-like hull. Consensus was high that there was no problem, and this was just another game of Mike's to get the Venturers to check out the area for safety.

"I think we'll go down to the shore and check it out from there," Mike said. "That should provide the answers for you."

"What's that weird building on the island off the southern point?" Mark asked.

Scott had read the tourist brochures on the area and decided to show off. "That's the Seal Rocks lighthouse built by convicts almost 200 years ago."

"So why such a large building under the lighthouse? It looks out of place," Steve chimed in.

"Remember Mike told us about the convicts who helped the local graziers in the area and also local businesses. Initially the Governor of the day built a permanent jail for the convicts to stay in while they worked for the local gentry," Scott offered. "Later, the jail was used for their most badly behaved within the Colony."

"What about the lighthouse?" asked Ian.

"Well, that was built around fifty years later, when the shipping trade picked up."

"Well done Scott, I'm glad someone has done their homework," Mike said.

"What about tours of the place? I've never seen a convict jail before, only the ones on TV," Steve said.

Peter took over the running of the conversation. "The State government used to conduct tours of the place but it started falling into disrepair about ten years ago," the chairman stated with authority.

Not to be outdone, Scott finished the story. "Apparently the government had thoughts of making it an island prison for today's worst criminals. My dad said there was a plan to make it like a mini-Alcatraz. However, dad said the humanitarians and civil liberties people got onto it before the last election and threatened to expose the plans. Dad said the Premier agreed to shelve the plans and since then, the place has gone to the rats."

"Well done Scott. I guess that answers that problem. Although it would be a great place to take our water pistols for a bit of urban warfare," Mike suggested.

The unit's style of urban warfare was nothing more than an elaborate game of hide-and-seek. Combatants on both sides used pump-action water pistols and balloons filled with water as weapons. It was a harmless game, but one the Venturers really loved. Mike drove the bus down to the beach area. The Venturers were filled with excitement at the prospect of riding out to the sub and checking it out for themselves.

"Alright lads, check out the water again from here," Mike said.

The waves were now pounding the shore heavily and the odd breaking section where the waves were rolling across the beach seemed even bigger.

"Steve, have look at the water now and tell me what you think?" Mike asked.

Steve had already scanned the beach on the way down from the headland. He knew it was too rough and unsafe for Mike to give the go-ahead.

"Well if I had a large boat, the sea would be fine." Steve dragged out his answer. "However, as it is, I seem to think it's too big for our boards."

Brett said he thought the boys could probably get past the first line of breakers but may find the going tough, especially trying to get on and off the sub. There was also a large rip running across the beach which could be a danger to any Venturer that may have been knocked off his board as he tried to breach the first line of waves. The boys begrudgingly saw the odds were against them for this adventure today. The consensus was to try the adventure another day when they could all enjoy it better.

"Next time we're in town I'll see whether we can get out to tour the old lighthouse, too," Mike suggested. "I'm not sure if we can, but I'll ask around and maybe the relevant government department may consider taking a group like ours on a tour."

Scott thought for a moment. "I'll try and ring dad tonight and see whether he can assist."

"Well done Scott," said Mike. "Police have amazing contacts and your good father should have heaps."

Peter asked around and it was decided to go into town for soft drinks and a round of junk food. Like teenagers around the world, once the Venturers had a sugar-fix through soft drinks, chocolates and lollies, they were fine. Mike then drove them back to camp where most went for a swim in the lake or played board games until dinner.

CHAPTER NINE

Over the horizon, the Pushkin was making its way steadily up the NSW coast. Four crew members had been specially selected to cut blocks of pure-grade heroin into a series of bundles and wrap them in waterproof material. The ten kilogram packets of heroin would supply the Sydney market for a short while and make millions of dollars in the process. The Chief Mate walked into the preparation room where the heroin was being organised.

"We'll be in position in two hours," he said to the four crewmen. "Make sure the packages are in the rubber boat, and it is ready to be launched at 0200 hours. I'll brief you further before you launch."

The sea swell had dropped after the southerly winds abated. This made it easier for the Pushkin to make good time and position itself off Seal Rocks. The First Mate briefed his drugs team at 0200 hours or 2 a.m. in ordinary time. He told them where the submarine was and how to secrete the packages. The mate then showed his four-man team diagrams of the partly submerged boat and indicated where the packages were to be placed. It all seemed like plain sailing from here.

The four men lowered the rubber ducky over the side and sped off from the Pushkin. Each of the men was wearing a black dive suit with booties. Goggles and snorkels in the tray of the boat completed the men's ensemble. The Pushkin was a couple of kilometres off Seal Rocks and it re-started its journey north at a slower rate of knots to allow the diving crew to lower their craft and make their way into the cove where the submarine lay waiting for them to drop their cargo and rejoin the ship.

The rubber ducky took around half an hour to reach the submarine. One crew member stayed onboard, maneuvering the small craft while the others went over the side and positioned their deadly cargo. One by one, the crewmen returned to the rubber boat and climbed aboard. Satisfied their work was done, the crew sped off to rejoin their ship. The whole operation took less than two hours.

"Were there any problems, comrades?" the First Mate asked his team as they doffed their wetsuits.

"No comrade. All went to plan and the parcels have been delivered," one of the team replied.

"Good, good. The Captain will be pleased. Best you change now and resume your shifts."

The First Mate made his way back to the operations room. He motioned to the Captain.

"Sir, all is well. The men have delivered the packages."

"Good, Ivan. I'll let the syndicate know," the Captain said.

"They will be pleased. Now we must move on. I feel we are being watched from above."

"Aye sir. The birds might be high, but we earthlings at least can track them too," the first mate said. "Our tracks must be covered."

"Well, Ivan, the good thing here is that Australia has no coast guard like the cursed Americans. Also, the Australian Navy is so small we shouldn't have a problem."

The Captain winked at his First Mate and returned to a large, opaque glass near a seated operator. It had a series of circles drawn in coloured ink and distances measured between them with a clock showing in the top, left-hand corner.

"We lost a bit of time when the rubber boat was launched and our slow down must have been noticed and tracked," the

Captain said without looking up from the screen. "We must make haste and start heading towards our next port."

"Is all in train for these packages to be picked up?" the First Mate asked.

"Yes all is in train. But you need not worry yourself with details. All is in train."

"We need an update of our position and timings for our next port."

"Aye sir."

Admiral Chris Ramage was the Australian Navy's Maritime Commander and his office had the best view of Sydney Harbour. He could watch the launch of the Sydney to Hobart yacht race unimpeded. He could also see every one of his naval vessels enter and leave port. This was quite handy, especially when he had to officiate at any arrival or departure ceremonies as he could see when ships were entering through the Sydney Heads or when the tugs were positioning themselves to tow ships into harbour.

"Tom is there any update on the Pushkin?" the Admiral asked.

"I'll check with Operations sir," the Lieutenant Commander said as he picked up the phone and started dialing.

"Robbie this is Lieutenant Commander David Giddings. Any update on the Pushkin?"

"Sir, it slowed down near Seal Rocks and then resumed her normal rate of knots," Lieutenant Jones replied.

"What about satellite imagery? Is there anything to suggest it did anything untoward or was it just engine problems?"

"Sir, we're looking into it and will have the latest pictures beamed to us shortly for decryption."

"Thanks, I'll let the boss know."

The Admiral was suspicious. The Pushkin affair, or 'Operation Stella', was a multi-agency operation and the Royal Australian Navy had to be seen to be on top of the situation. Ramage reached for the phone and rang the head of Naval Intelligence, Rear Admiral Drew Curry, an old classmate.

"Drew, its Chris. What's the latest on the Pushkin?" Ramage asked.

"Chris! It's been too long between conferences. My people believe the Pushkin underwent some routine maintenance and then pushed on," Rear Admiral Curry replied. "There are no populated areas onshore near where it stopped."

"Where did it heave to Drew?"

"Just off the Seal Rocks lighthouse. It only stopped momentarily and then continued."

"Thanks Drew. If anything turns up please call me. I have the Chief of the Defence Force breathing down my neck enquiring whether we should launch a patrol boat or destroyer to intercept the Pushkin. He's being harangued by the Federal police and the Prime Minister's Department, never mind Coastwatch. Phew!"

"Chris, I'll let you know the moment we have something."

The two Admirals rang off.

CHAPTER TEN

Sunrises and sunsets on Myall Lake where the Venturers were camped, were generally spectacular. This day was no exception. Scott had stirred early and couldn't get back to sleep. He decided to get up and have a cup of tea and have a quiet moment of solitude.

"Good morning Scott," Mike said as he lifted his head from under the trestle table.

"Morning Mike," Scott replied.

"Another top day ahead by the look of it."

Scott moved closer to the table and then realised Mike was adjusting the table's legs. Mike looked up and smiled.

"I couldn't sleep either. I don't know why I'm restless, probably the thought of our swim today. That is, if the sea is calmer."

Mike stood up and reached for his mug.

"I just love the beautiful colours of the sky and the cool breeze of the early mornings," Scott said as he reached for the tea bags.

"So do I," Mike answered. "Whenever I have bivouacked with the army in central Australia, I have been almost overawed by the shows put on by Mother Nature, and of course, they were just for me."

"Such as?" Scott asked.

"Well, I'll always remember my first night in the Northern Territory. It was so hot no one erected any hutchies. We just slept on our stretchers out in the open. Watching the stars was simply amazing.

"In our city environs we only get to see clutches of stars because of the city lights. Out there, away from the city, there were millions of stars. It was also fantastic to watch so many shooting stars stream overhead."

Scott had boiled the billy on the stove and was making them both their first cup of tea of the day.

"What about the clouds? Surely they would have hidden most of the stars?"

A smile started to appear on Mike's face.

"No. Reality is there are hardly any clouds where I went. That's why the area is called the Red Centre. The soil is so red and dry. You'll have to go there one day and take in the sights. The sunsets were to die for. I know you love art so I'll describe them for you.

"Imagine there is a huge, opaque glass covering the sky, and behind it is a huge light that sends rays of various warm colours," Mike started.

"Now think about the glass cracking in long fingers or shards and allowing an array of light blues, pinks, reds, oranges and yellow to stream through. The movement of the light is very subtle and as it intensifies it starts dropping the blues and pinks and increases the reds and oranges.

"The shards withdraw, and left in place is a huge, orange sun sitting on a bed of red horizon. Slowly the sun drops down through the horizon and disappears. The orange and red are then replaced by the appearance of light and dark blue as the sun sinks below our gaze, leaving us with twilight and then night."

"Wow Mike!" Scott was enthralled. His tea was in his hand, but he was too entranced by Mike's descriptive prowess to take a sip in case he broke the spell.

"I've got to get there and see the sunsets, stars and even the crocodiles for myself," Scott said. "Maybe we could organise a Venturer camp to Timber Creek where the asteroid hit the Earth all those eons ago."

"Funny you should mention Timber Creek, Scott," Mike said as he watched is young charge. "I once had to camp there for two weeks with the Regular Army and ended up playing helicopter-tag with a Major General."

"What haven't you done?" Scott asked.

"I haven't done a lot of things, but I don't believe in waiting around for my future. I believe in making it as I go."

Other Venturers started to stir as the drone of conversation reached into their sub consciousness and told them Mike was up and getting ready for the next adventure.

CHAPTER ELEVEN

Vitali and the others had enjoyed their drive up the Pacific Highway from Sydney to Myall Lakes. They had driven directly to a headland overlooking the partly-submerged submarine.

"When do you want to retrieve our packages?" Dimitri asked Vitali.

"There is no need to hurry. No one's going to get them, except us," the team leader replied.

"I think we need a few hours' sleep so we're more than fresh for the long drive back, comrade!"

"Mmm. Not too many hours," Dimitri replied.

"No. Just a few. This will allow us better access to the sub when the tide is lower and more light to see by," Vitali said.

"Okay, comrade. This is your show," Dimitri reminded his leader.

Vitali looked at his lieutenant. "We also have to appear to be normal divers so we don't attract unnecessary attention."

Vitali and his team drove back to the main township and found the motel they had booked into as a standby. 'The sleep will also help calm the team members,' Vitali thought.

Dimitri took a different viewpoint, but said nothing to his team leader. He believed the Russian team should have recovered the packages as soon as they arrived - under the cover of darkness. They could have departed before the sun was too high and headed back to Sydney to deliver their white powder of addiction and death. He decided to keep guard while the others slept.

CHAPTER TWELVE

Brett had a very light sleep. His excitement about going on the sub was hard for him to contain. Eventually, he had to get out of his warm sleeping bag and go to the toilet. The call of nature was more powerful now than the call of sleep. He checked his watch and saw it was only 5.30 a.m. No one in their right minds would be up so early? Then again ...

'No, he doesn't get up this early ... does he?' Brett thought as he wondered whether Mike was up. Brett checked the dining tent and saw no lights on. He was about to go back to bed when Mike came into the tent armed with his mug.

"Morning Brett! You're up pretty early aren't you?"

"Hi Mike. I couldn't sleep. It must have been all the cordial or coffee I drank last night," Brett replied.

Mike looked at his young charge and realised what had happened. "A bit excited about the sub Brett?"

Brett looked agog. 'Was this guy a mind reader or something?'

"Yes, I suppose so. I was dreaming again of captaining the sub and taking it for a spin off the coast," Brett said as his face began to light up with a smile. "Mind you, I brought it back in one piece."

Both laughed.

"Well done Scott. I always like a man that can deliver," Mike said. "Let's get our first brew."

"What about you Mike? Why are you up so early?" Brett asked.

"For some unknown reason my body clock is set for around 5 a.m. The moment there is light in the sky I feel the call to wake up, then I find I can't go back to sleep. If I do try and force myself I find I then want to sleep most of the day. The problem is at night then when I can't get to sleep because I've had too much already, and so on."

Mike started filling a billy with water from the large, plastic water barrel. Scott had found the gas lighter and had ignited the gas stove ready for the billy.

"I still say this is the best part of the day," Mike said. "Shortly, the sun will start sending its fingers of light racing across the sky. The wind will drop in awe and the wildlife will either scurry for cover if they are nocturnal or start waking up."

Scott picked up on the story.

"Then the dark blobs on the horizon start blinking as the humans begin their working day by turning on their house lights," he continued. "The quiet becomes disturbed as the wave of human movement takes over from the subtle meanderings of the animal kingdom ...."

"Well done Scott! That was great. Have you ever thought about becoming a writer when you are older?" Mike asked.

"I love English at school, and I enjoy writing essays. It just gets hard sometimes because dad is not switched on for it, being a cop, and writing is not Mum's forte."

Mike looked knowingly at Scott and smiled. "Writing does not come from your parents but from within your very being. It should be an extension of your mind and more importantly, your imagination."

Scott took in what Mike said and knew he was right. The drive to tell a yarn, a story, came from within. It was in-built in some people, like a homing beacon for bats.

"So what is the plan for today?" Scott asked.

"We'll make an early start and be at the sub site by 8.00 a.m. By the time we unload, get ready and actually get in the water, it should be around 8.30 a.m." Mike continued, "This way we beat the rising tide on the way out."

"Mike, what if the surf is rough again today ... do we go in?" Scott asked.

"No. I'm not prepared to risk it. Your lives mean more to me than exploring some old submarine that will still be here next time there is a calm tide."

Each of them made a cup of coffee and then sat back to watch nature at play.

CHAPTER THIRTEEN

The computer beeped as it received the latest message from Maritime Command. The Navy commander studied the images, printed two copies and then forwarded the message to his boss, Rear Admiral Chris Ramage. The Commander picked up the phone.

"Sir, may I see you please? MHQ has done an analysis of satellite imagery surrounding our Russian friends," he said. "It looks like they've been up to something."

"You had better come straight in – and bring the imagery," the Admiral answered.

"Aye, sir."

The commander grabbed his images and paperwork and headed to his boss's office.

"Sir, I forwarded Commander Barnes's imagery and memo to you," Commander O'Shea informed his boss. "I have also printed out a copy of the satellite image of the ship. It seems that when it was off Myall Lakes it disembarked a rib (rigid inflatable boat) with four people aboard."

"The question now is what did they do? Did they drop off any drugs or arms or other materials? And if so, where?" the Admiral wondered. "Are there any landmarks, bridges or small islands near where they stopped?"

"Sir, Operations is checking that now. Would you like to see the satellite imagery?"

"Yes Chris. Run it through the overhead projector in the meeting room."

"Aye, sir."

Commander O'Shea readied the meeting room. It was here a number of recent major operations by Australian forces had been planned. Today would only be the beginning of intense preparation for this particular homeland problem.

Commander O'Shea knew it was touch and go between Defence Headquarters and the Prime Minister's office as to how far Defence would continue monitoring the Pushkin before other government agencies took over.

"What time was this image of the Pushkin taken?" the Admiral enquired.

"Sir, around 0100 hours today," Commander O'Shea replied.

"The Pushkin slowed down to allow the rib to be taken off. You can see the outline of four people carrying some packages, dressed in what looks to be wetsuits."

"Drugs or explosives do you reckon?" the Admiral asked.

"Sir, the Pushkin so far hasn't been involved in anything of a direct terrorist nature. Our assumption and that of Maritime Command, is that the crew are involved in other acts of skullduggery – more than likely drugs."

"Chris, call Inspector Farrell of the Federal Police and ask him to come in for a brief and a chat will you? I think it is time the Feds took a closer interest in this case," the Admiral said.

"Will do sir. I'll check with your secretary and see what times you are available."

Commander O'Shea returned to his office and rang the Federal police.

"Chris, thanks for the call," Inspector Farrell said. "We've been monitoring the Pushkin for some time, but we have had nothing concrete to act upon."

"No problems David. If our imagery verifies what I've told you this should place you in the box seat," Commander O'Shea said.

"Not quite. If the packages were contraband, how long would it take you to intercept the Pushkin and approximately where?"

"Dave, I'll get an analysis done before you see the Admiral this afternoon."

"Thanks Chris. I'll find out what we have available to stop our friends as well."

Admiral Ramage dialled Superintendent Clive Hartcher at Customs.

"Clive I may have to intercept the Pushkin and arrest her. We have some satellite imagery that shows four of her crew boarded a rib early today and dropped off some packages. We don't know where the ship's rib took the four, but we are checking. I'll send over some images."

Superintendent Hartcher replaced his phone in his receiver. He moved to the main conference table in his office and started studying the map of the New South Wales coast where the Pushkin had travelled. He knew most of the coastline between the Victorian border in the south and the Queensland border in the north.

"So what were these mongrels after? What made them go near Myall Lakes? There's nothing there," he said to himself. He turned to his computer and called up a search engine. Myall Lakes. Only local council information came on screen. He checked the local history page and sat glued to his screen. Superintendent Hartcher only had a small role to play in the Pushkin affair. He would love to have a fleet of purpose-built Customs ships with 50 calibre machine guns mounted on their side railings and maybe six-inch guns mounted up forward. However, he knew he was dreaming.

Successive Australian governments had baulked at the notion of arming the Customs department with the big toys. A new wind was beginning to blow in the electorate as the Navy indicated it may relinquish its current role in homeland border and contraband protection to Customs. This would leave the Navy free to intercept illegal ships straying into Australia's special fishing zones and also freed the fleet to monitor foreign naval ships as they sailed anywhere near the island continent. Both major political parties in Australia saw the need to scale up the role of Customs following the 911 terrorist strikes on New York, thereby freeing the Navy to undertake its traditional role. Both political parties were half-heartedly talking about increasing the role of Customs, adding well-armed ships to its tiny fleet and allowing the service to play a greater role. Superintendent Hartcher knew any political turnaround would take time – time to educate the voting population about the need for the expansion of the service and in turn create a desire for change in time for the next election. He began to check his coastline maps.

'Why would the Pushkin have stopped near Myall Lakes? A great holiday place. Pristine environment; national park.'

It was an area where one Australian prime minister used to take his family on holidays. Hartcher pondered the clues as an aide brought him a cup of coffee. He picked up his coffee the same moment as his eyes made contact with a tourist map of Myall Lakes. He started laughing. He reached for the phone then realised he was trying to dial with a cup of coffee in his hands. A chuckle rang out in his office as he put his coffee down and reached for the phone again.

"Chris, it's Clive Hartcher. I know where the Russians went! Why – I don't know. However I'm pretty sure it was the old wrecked submarine in the area. There's nothing else there except a lighthouse and that's currently empty."

The conversation between Admiral Ramage and Superintendent Hartcher was brief. Both men rang off. Admiral

Ramage called his aide-de-camp, Lieutenant Jim Barndon, into his office.

"Jim, have Captain Potter from HMAS Penguin call me urgently," the Admiral ordered. "Better still, tell him to come over here pronto and ring me en route."

"Aye sir," Lieutenant Barndon replied.

Within a minute the Captain had dialled the admiral's office.

"Sir, Captain Potter is on the other line," Lieutenant Barndon announced.

"Good. Put him through, thanks Jim."

"Jeff?"

"Sir, long time, no hear."

The Admiral told him to think about one of his former boats, HMAS Otway.

"She's lying offshore from Myall Lakes I believe. Foundered during a large storm when she was on her way to Japan for scrap," Captain Potter recalled.

"Yes. She's still there. But could she prove a risk if she falls into the hands of terrorists?" the Admiral asked.

"No sir. She was heavily gutted before being sold to scrap. The Otway should be nothing more than a diver's retreat and a fish growth area."

"We have a small problem and I need your advice," Admiral Ramage said. "Think about where you could possibly hide things on her today and I'll see you in my office shortly."

"Aye sir."

CHAPTER FOURTEEN

"Peter what's the torch for? Night's over," Scott asked when he saw the unit chairman walking towards he and Mike.

"Mr Smarty Pants, it may be sunny here but where we are going may have some dark holes and crevices," Peter said with a look of annoyance.

"You can't get in the sub ... it's all closed up and sealed," Scott said.

"Yes, but I want to check her out as much as I can."

"Good idea Peter," Mike said.

"Are the elastic-sided headlamps we use around the camp any good for our swim?" Scott asked.

"No," Peter said definitely. "They'll work okay for a little while and then when the water seeps into the seals they'll stop and your parents, or you, are up for a new one!"

"Just lucky mine is a diver's torch – I think. I'll check it out first."

Mike looked at them both. "It's time we woke our sleeping beauties and ripped into some brekky. We have to make sure all our gear is right. Also we have to ensure we have some good rations to come back to including a gas stove to make a hot brew," Mike said.

CHAPTER FIFTEEN

"Dimitri! Wake up. We must start moving before it gets too late," Vitali urged. He yelled to the others to start getting ready.

"What about breakfast?" Boris asked.

"Afterwards. If we eat now, before we go to the sub you will just be feeding the fish, because you'll be sick with all the movement in the boat," Vitali said.

"Vitali! Check the weapons. Boris! Get the dive suits ready."

"Da, boss!"

The men moved methodically as if their actions were orchestrated. They were accustomed to obeying orders and using the equipment. They did not like to make mistakes. Vitali was pleased, at least, with the experience of his team. This would make the job quicker so he could go home faster. He didn't like the thought of dealing with the drug scum of Cabramatta. They were the real criminals. Vitali believed in conspiracy theories. In his heart, he believed the police and government had conspired to push the State capital's drug problem into a narrow corner of the city's southwest. This allowed Sydney's upper and middle class kids a form of protection when the police came down hard on drug operators elsewhere in the city.

In Cabramatta, the police took a softer approach, resulting in the dealers being pushed into a small area of operation. This style of policing allowed for greater observation of the drug dealers and their clients as they only had a small area to work in.

"Vitali, the boat operator has had some engine trouble," Boris announced. "Apparently, someone stole the engine on the boat we had booked and now he has to find a replacement."

"Who can you trust these days?" Vitali asked, a wry smile emerging across his face.

"How long before we can go?"

"He's hoping within the hour."

Vitali felt a cold shiver go down his spine. This was an omen – maybe.

CHAPTER SIXTEEN

"Come on, let's go! Our sub's waiting," Peter started yelling at his Venturers. "We want to beat the tide."

Mike and Scott gave each other a knowing smile and went to their tents to dress. They emerged within a few minutes and started eating their breakfasts. Today there was no hearty meal of sausages, bacon, eggs and tomatoes, instead, only cereal and fruit. Mike had gone over today's plan in detail with the older Venturers last night. He watched with glee as the older boys roused the younger ones and kept everyone moving. This even extended to the production of sandwiches for when they came out of the water. Mike believed the boys would take a couple of hours to paddle out to the sub and explore it fully before paddling back to the beach.

"Scott, ensure we have the first aid kit packed. Also, make sure the tool box is brought too, it's in the gear tent."

"I'm on it Mike," Scott answered. He never questioned Mike about being asked to do jobs like this as it was all in a day's work for the betterment of the unit.

"Ensure you have something warm to put on once you return to the bus," Peter said. "You may not notice the cold at first but you'll certainly feel it afterwards if you don't dress properly."

Steve orchestrated a combined response, "YES DAD!" The boys laughed as Peter turned bright red.

"I don't mind if you ignore your chairman," Mike told the boys. "But, if you get cold after our little swim, don't come crying to me! I'll suddenly develop deafness and won't be able to hear you as you shiver and get all miserable." Mike watched the expressions change on the boys faces.

Scott did all he could to stop from laughing. He knew who had the upper hand – also the experience. He helped pack the collection of body boards and surfboards into the trailer. This was going to be a day he would never forget.

Scott felt energised at the thought of sharing the experience with his fellow Venturers, and of course Mike. Today's style of adventure was right out of a Boy's Own annual, and he was here to share it. No! He was here to live it! Scott thought how he would love to have shared the experience with his brother Brad. However, this was never to be as Brad didn't enjoy Venturer-type activities. He was more the outgoing type with the girls.

"Mike, we're ready to go when you are," Peter said.

"All the equipment stowed?" Mike asked.

"Aye, mon capitán," Peter replied in a pirate's voice.

Mike took up the theme, "Avast you landlubbers! It's the top of the tide and we must be off. For those non-pirates among you who watch American TV shows - let's haul ass!"

The boys laughed as they stepped onto the bus. Peter counted the boys in while Steve did a quick security check of the camp to ensure all the tents were zippered close. Mark did a quick visual check of the site to ensure no valuables, such as cameras or mobile phones were left lying around. Mike had a good routine with the older boys shepherding and looking after the younger ones.

"All secure, mon capitán," Steve said to Mike as he boarded.

"All okay our Captain," Mark said with a huge grin.

"Avast! All is well, mon capitán. We can proceed," Peter replied as he climbed into the front passenger seat.

Mike closed the bus door and started driving the boys to an adventure they would always remember.

The noise level in the bus was high as the boys talked excitedly among themselves. A few divers' torches flashed as the boys checked them.

"First, they were pirates and now they are characters from Star Wars," Peter commented to Mike.

"Welcome to a boy's world of adventure and fantasy! Maybe what we have here is space pirates trapped in teenage boys' bodies."

Peter looked at Mike and smiled. 'This will be a good day.'

Mike found a sandy parking area on the approach to the beach that would accommodate his mini bus and trailer.

"Peter and Mark, check out the surf and hurry back," Mike ordered. "If it is too rough for the younger ones to paddle, we'll go elsewhere for the day."

"Okay Mike," Peter answered as the two boys started running over a sand hill and onto the beach.

It was a fantastic sight in front of them. The ocean had calmed and the submarine could easily be seen in the far distance. The boys made their way back to the bus. Mike had already got the other Venturers organised with most of the boogie boards and surf paddle boards already out of the trailer. The area around the bus was a hive of activity as the boys readied themselves.

"It's like a mill pond out there," Peter said. "It shouldn't take too long to get to the sub."

"Thanks Peter. Okay everyone, listen to me," Mike announced.

This is where Mike came into his own. He gave instructions for each Venturer to pair off and ensure their mate was okay. The boys' level of excitement was high. They locked the bus and trailer, gathered their boards and made their way over the sand hill and onto the beach.

CHAPTER SEVENTEEN

Dimitri replaced the phone on the receiver.

"He'll have another boat fuelled and ready to go in about twenty minutes," he informed Boris.

"Maybe we can hurry him along a bit. Get your gear and let's get to the wharf."

"Okay. But by the way this man talks, I don't think he'll move any faster."

Vitali drove the car to the wharf and couldn't help noticing how quiet it was – he started grinning. Gone were the endless lines of traffic around Moscow and the heavily-dressed comrades warding off sub zero temperatures as they went to work. Vitali knew he was in an Australian holiday destination but he couldn't get used to the lack of people and activity. He nodded to himself as he thought how backward the Aussies must be. After all, where were the armed police and soldiers patrolling the port and streets? He now understood why his mafia bosses decided to hit Australia – it was easy pickings.

"Dimitri, how long to go now?" Boris asked.

"He should be here in five minutes."

"Okay. Let's hope no other thieves stole his craft."

The men looked at each other and laughed. Finally a small outboard could be seen rounding the point and heading towards the boatshed. The small, black and white craft looked as if it was built to go anywhere on the seas. Its engines gurgled as it drew nearer to the international visitors.

"Hi folks, sorry for the delay," the boat's skipper said. "Bloody thieves stole the red boat I prepared for you yesterday. Never mind, this one is faster and the owner has thrown in a six pack for you," the man said with a grin.

Boris smiled and thanked the skipper while quickly ushering his team onto the boat with their gear.

"So, where are you going? Off the point to dive? Or further out to sea for a fish?"

Dimitri helped the skipper from his boat and started to head for the wheelhouse. None of the Russians answered. The boat started pulling away from the wharf when the skipper yelled out, "If you're going near the sub be careful. I saw a group of surfers heading out that way."

It was too late. Boris and his men were in too big a rush. They only heard the skipper start talking before their craft was moving and rapidly picking up speed. One of the men asked Boris what the man had said. Boris hadn't heard the whole message either.

"I think there is some Aussie beer onboard," Boris said. "Look for a six pack – whatever that is."

The men had a quick look around the boat and found a plastic icebox with six beers inside.

"Not yet," Boris cautioned. "Wait until we have our love packages. The beer will help us celebrate."

The craft effortlessly lifted its bow and soared through the water. This was a perfect day for boating – a cloudless sky, calm sea and no wind. The Russians wasted no time in donning their wetsuits. Two of the men strapped large diving knives to their thighs. The other two loaded spear guns. Each of them put on their booties and grabbed their fins from the dive bags.

CHAPTER EIGHTEEN

Scott was on a high. This was adventure! Paddling out to a submarine and exploring it would be something he would tell his own children about.

"Keep together!" Peter shouted. "Bunch up and keep checking your mate. We don't want any stragglers out here."

Mike looked around and nodded. Peter would make a good army officer. He was a good leader – a natural leader.

"Shark! Shark!" Mark yelled as he pointed to some grey fins plying through the water towards them around one hundred metres out to sea. A scare cut through the Venturers like an electric shock. Two of the boys fell off their boards and started gulping water. Scott tried to kneel on his board to get a better view. There were now three fins in sight and heading right towards the boys! Mike started raising his hand in anticipation of telling the boys to bunch up. Scott noticed the large school of fish heading towards the group. Suddenly, fear gave way to exhilaration and laughing.

"They're dolphins!" Scott shouted. "It's a pod of dolphins chasing some small fish. We're okay. Wherever there is a pod of dolphins, there are usually no sharks!"

Mike looked at Mark and Peter.

"I knew that," he said as he started to smile. "Good one Scott."

The older boys let go of their anxiety too and picked up on what Mike yelled out to them.

"Good one Scott!" they shouted in chorus and then they all started laughing.

Scott swallowed hard and went back to paddling. 'This was going to be a very good day,' he thought. The dolphins kept their distance but kept in view of the boys. This was an interesting collection of humans in the dolphins' playground. Some of the dolphins chased the school of fish, while others swam near the boys for a closer view. The gap between the boys and the submarine was closing. The sea was slight and a cool breeze picked up.

CHAPTER NINETEEN

The calls between Maritime Headquarters, the Federal and State police and Customs became more frequent. Satellites were now relaying the coordinates of the Pushkin after every flyover. These were being plotted by Navy and Customs staff and sent to the police. Inspector Dave Farrell hated drug runners. His favourite niece was mysteriously found dead in a worker's hut beside a river a few months after she had disappeared. The girl was a drug addict and about to be a prime witness for the prosecution in an upcoming trial. She was found dead with a syringe in her arm. The trial was aborted, as the only credible witness was now dead.

Inspector Farrell sat uneasy. He wanted the Russian drug runners caught and their cache found. However, he was hamstrung as to exactly what they did when they released their inflatable raft. Also, if the raft returned to the Pushkin what was its mission? And did it leave anything or anyone behind? The phone rang and his attention was immediately refocused.

"Dave, its Chris Hartcher, long time – no fish."

"Too right Chris! The powers that be have kept you and I away from our scaly friends," Inspector Farrell replied.

"Dave, I think I know where our friends went last night," Inspector Hartcher said to his old fishing mate. "Do you remember the Navy submarine being towed to Japan for scrap that broke its lines during a storm and washed up near a beach?"

"Yeah, that was awhile ago though."

"I've checked the maritime maps for that area of the coast and they may have been heading towards Myall Lakes where the sub foundered. There's a nice cove there and an old colonial prison and lighthouse nearby at Seal Rocks. My guess is the crew came ashore near the sub and dropped off some dope before rejoining the Pushkin."

Dave Farrell thought for a moment. "I think you're right. The area would be a smuggler's delight. I'll send a crew to the area pronto. What about the Navy?"

"I spoke with Admiral Ritchie earlier and he thinks they have dropped off some dope on the sub. He's sending a dive crew to the area."

"Why the sub? It's a long way from shore for dope addicts to swim to and retrieve their packages of death."

Chris Hartcher thought for few moments. "Unless ... they planned to use a boat to pick up their gear. If I remember correctly, there is only one boat operator that hires out craft in that area. He could be worth a check."

Dave Farrell was a man of action. Within seconds of replacing the phone receiver he was on his computer looking up boat operators using the electronic version of the white pages. Ten minutes later, he was back on the phone to Inspector Hartcher.

"Chris, good news. A group of thugs hired a speed boat early this morning to go fishing for the day," Farrell said.

"They took dive bags with them to snorkel in the area."

"What time did they pick up the boat?"

"Around 8.30 a.m. Apparently they are pretty heavy-set men with a look as though they were from a northern hemisphere winter."

"Chris, it has to be them! What time will you have someone in the area?"

"Probably within the hour. Once we get radio coverage with the car in the Myall Lakes area, we'll make a beeline to the boat hire place."

The two men rang off. Myall Lakes was reasonably accessible for cars, but radio and telephone relay towers dotted along the highway were a long way from the pristine bush and lakes district. Campers loved the area. Mobile phones did not work because of the lack of network coverage. This was bliss for partners of business people who were accustomed to using the devices on a monotonously regular level. Police cars were no different. If the driver had no reception on his mobile phone, then chances were, the police radio was out of range too.

CHAPTER TWENTY

Headquarters Australian Theatre was busy working with Maritime Command organising support for the warship being ordered by Navy to intercept the Pushkin. Maritime Command knew its sailors onboard the ship weren't trained for possible anti-terrorist threats. Calculations were being conducted by Operations staff to see whether it was feasible for a helicopter to take a section of Special Air Service Regiment (SASR) soldiers from the mainland to board the ship. The trouble was, the SASR soldiers were based in Sydney and the helicopters in Queensland.

Once the helicopter had dropped the soldiers onboard the Pushkin it would fly around the ship to give air support. The moment the ship was secured, the helicopter would fly to the warship and land on its flight deck. Ribbed, inflatable boats would then be sent to the Pushkin from the warship to recover the soldiers. Then armed sailors would take over and sail the Pushkin to Sydney, with the crew secured below decks.

The plan had to be put together and the various federal and state agencies needed to be briefed. The commander of the SASR in Sydney warned his men as they started packing their kit in preparation. Two Black Hawk helicopters were ordered to fly to Sydney for their SASR cargo. Police were liaised with to ensure that when the green light was given by the Federal government for the SASR to go in, then police pursuit cars could organise a clear traffic corridor to the airport. The chink in the plan was proof the Russians had actually done something illegal. The proof was still to be discovered.

CHAPTER TWENTY-ONE

The Venturers had made good timing when paddling out to the submarine. Mike and Peter had a good look at their unit, as each of the boys started to tie their boards to the other. The nose of each board had a double rubber strap. The boys simply looped their straps together with the last one tying his off.

"They look like tired little puppies," Peter said to Mike.

"Ah yes, but very excited to be here."

Mike was worried about the return trip. The excitement should give way to weariness and lethargy – hopefully not to mistakes.

"Mark, you stay with one group. Peter you take the second and Mark take the third. I'll float between all three and act as a shepherd in case anyone becomes injured."

The three answered in chorus as one, "AYE, MY CAPTAIN!"

Scott was the first to successfully climb the outer hull. The other boys had tried but had slipped off the boat because of the moss caked on the boat's skin. Each of the boys wore running shoes or boating-type shoes, however, the rubber soles never had much of a chance against the moss. Scott made his way gingerly to the main deck. The swell had slowly started to pick up and buffet the boys and the boat with small waves.

"Greg, hold onto something or ...," Mike was cut off in mid-sentence when the stocky youth slipped from the side of the boat and went under. The action appeared in slow motion in

Mike's head as he saw Greg turn to say something and then slip backwards into the sea.

Within a few moments, Greg was back on the surface with a huge grin. 'Welcome to the challenge of Venturers,' Mike thought.

The other boys weren't faring too well either. Scott slowly made his way onto the deck to where Greg was swimming.

"Greg, try a bit further down. It's pretty slippery but you should make it," Scott yelled out.

Mike looked up and saw a blonde crop of hair on deck and knew immediately who it was.

"Well done Scott! I should have known you'd be the first," Mike yelled as he paddled between groups of Venturers.

Within a few moments, a couple more crops of hair could be seen on the boat's deck as more Venturers found their way up the slimy hull. Four of the boys had managed to climb onto the deck of the submarine. It was pretty hard going now, not because the sea had risen to a large swell or a big wind was blowing. No – the boys were having so much fun trying to get aboard and falling back into the water they kept laughing so much.

Mark was the first. He had been trying to climb over one of the rear planes when his hand pushed onto something odd. He had worn swimming goggles used by competitive swimmers and was able to see under the surface without much trouble.

"Mike, have a look at this," Mark said excitedly.

He wasn't sure whether he done the right thing or not. Mike swam over to Mark and immediately picked up the tension in the boy.

"What's up mate?" Mike asked.

"Mike, I think this sub is going to be blown up and we should leave here now!" Mark said speedily.

"Slow down," Mike said. "This is not like you. What's wrong?"

Mark raised his right hand from under the water and showed Mike the rectangular package wrapped in waterproof material.

"Is this C4 explosive material?" Mark asked nervously.

"Well if it was, you'd be lucky to still have your arm."

"Wherever you dislodged it from would have exploded," Mike said.

The army Captain checked out the package.

"Mark, I think we have stumbled onto something far bigger than explosives. Say nothing. Swim over to Peter and Greg and tell them to come here pronto without causing any alarm."

"Yes sir!" Mark swam off to gather the other patrol leaders while Mike examined the package.

He didn't want to open it for fear it could contaminate any evidence. Within a couple of minutes his patrol leaders were bobbing in the water around him.

"Has anyone else found any packages like these?" Mike asked as he raised the waterproof rectangle from the water.

"I think Brett has one, and also Ian," Peter replied.

"Why didn't you call me? They could be explosives!" Mike asked heatedly.

"Mike, they have only just found them, as we were told to see you," Peter said.

"Sorry, Chairman. I think they could be drugs or something else that's nasty. We better round up the boys and ...."

Before Mike could finish Scott yelled that there was a speedboat heading towards the sub.

"Let me handle this everyone. Peter, Mark, get as many packages as you can and keep them out of sight. If things don't turn out well, drop them and let them sink."

"That will be hard," Mark answered. "They float."

"Quickly gather everyone together at their boards," Mike said.

The boys swam off and started calling for the other Venturers to get off the sub and back onto their boards. There was a great deal of resistance as the boys were having a lot of fun.

CHAPTER TWENTY-TWO

"We should be in sight of the submarine around the next cove," Vitali told Dimitri. "It's not far now."

"I hope no one is sightseeing around the sub, that could pose us a problem," Dimitri replied.

Vitali and Boris patted their dive bags.

"No problems boss. Both Smith and Wesson will look after them. What's left will be finished off by the sharks," Vitali assured him.

The men laughed as they reached for their goggles and snorkels. Their boat had made good time so far, but the men were anxious to recover their booty and slip back into the main traffic throng to Sydney and anonymity. Here they were exposed and stood out. Vitali was already calculating how he would spend his rubles. He knew his mafia dons wouldn't allow him to stay in Australia. His mission was to retrieve the drugs, sell them, transfer the money to a registered international bank account and go home to Moscow.

Dimitri was worried about the sale of the drugs and how long it would take to actually turn the white powder of death into money. Hopefully it would only take a few days. He wanted to see more of Sydney on this, his third trip. Every time he had been to the New South Wales capital it was only for a few days. He remembered the quaint Customs officer at Sydney airport asking him whether he was visiting for business or pleasure.

"Business," was the stock reply. This was quite truthful as the pleasure would come later when another batch of drugs had been sold and the next group of junkies were affected by the Russian white powder of self-destruction to hit the streets. A strong breeze picked up and sprayed the Russians with water.

"Vitali, this is not quite like the Volga, is it?" Boris asked.

"This country is too young. The people here haven't put as many chemicals and pollution into their water as we have – give them time."

The men laughed as the convict lighthouse came into view. They gazed intently at the large, imposing sandstone structure. It had two storeys of flat structure and sticking out from one end was a giant lighthouse. A jetty stood near the end of the lighthouse, jutting into the bay. At the base of the lighthouse a road wound around to the jetty and off into the national park. No cars were parked near the keeper's hut, nor any boat tied to the jetty. It looked deserted.

"And they call us barbaric with our prisons," Boris said. "At least we had something for our prisoners to do, whether it was working in the gulags or defence installations like Smirnsk."

"Comrade, nothing much changes, just the countryside," Dimitri said. "Remember, these buildings are from the time the British capitalist pigs ran this place. It was quite some time before the Australians took over management."

"Boss, we should get ready. Once we clear these heads the sub is only a few minutes away in the next cove," Vitali reminded Dimitri.

"You are right, of course Vitali. Okay, everyone, get prepared to be wet and retrieve our love packages," Dimitri announced.

"Dimitri, come quick!" Vitali said. "I think the Australian Navy is waiting for us!"

Dimitri clambered forward on the small boat and took the binoculars. "What the ...? Wait! They are children – not sailors. They're just boys. No weapons."

"Dimitri, what if they have our packages?"

"Take them from them and get rid of the kids. We can't afford to have witnesses around."

Boris couldn't stand loose ends. In his mind's eye he could see a herd of parents and police chasing his group and stopping them from boarding their aircraft to Moscow.

"Dimitri, there are too many of them to arrange a swimming 'accident'," Boris said.

"We can shoot them where they are and tie their bodies to the sub. That will at least buy us time to return to Sydney before anyone sees us," Dimitri decided, as he became more infuriated.

"Get your weapons ready!"

Vitali watched eagerly as the Venturers grouped together. His eyes went from boy to boy and then lingered on Mike. He watched as the Venturer leader organised the boys to get back on their boards. Mike was sitting on his boogie board ensuring the boys had mounted theirs and untied all the leads to allow for independent movement back to shore. He noticed the speedboat racing closer and he felt totally vulnerable. What started out as a great day of adventure was starting to turn into a problem.

"Boris, drive the boat around the sub slowly while we round up these boys," Dimitri ordered.

"Da!" came Boris's reply.

Dimitri rounded on Boris and pointed his handgun at his offsider's chest.

"Speak only English .... got it?" Dimitri said tersely.

"Yes boss ... a momentary slip."

Dimitri nodded and then went to the port side of the boat as it came within shouting distance of the submarine.

"Good morning," Mike said as the boat came level with him and the boys.

"Good morning," Dimitri replied. "Having a good time on the sub?"

"Yes it's been great, but we have to get back for lunch ... we have some people expecting us," Mike said.

"Did you find anything unusual around the sub?" Dimitri asked.

"Like what? Plenty of slimy seaweed and a heap of fish ... that's about all."

Boris gently drove the boat around the boys while Vitali and Dimitri looked for the packages.

"Did you find any ...."

Before he could finish speaking, a package Peter was holding slipped out of his hands and surfaced in front of him. Dimitri and Vitali pointed their handguns at the Venturers.

"What is that? A slimy piece of seaweed?" Dimitri asked brusquely. "Where are the rest of them?"

Mike went pale. Everyone's worst nightmare had started to materialise. His charges weren't only in danger of the sea and all it held, but now, three gangsters!

"We don't know what you are talking about. Whatever that is, it's not ours," Mike said.

"Too right it's not yours," Dimitri said. "What others do you have? Tell me now and I may let you live."

Mike looked at the Venturers. They were becoming tense and unnerved with these people pointing weapons at them. He opted for a lifeline.

"Look, I don't know who you are or what you want. These boys are all Scouts just out to explore the submarine. We're not hiding anything and we have nothing that's yours. Please let us go and we'll be on our way."

Vitali finished putting his fins, mask and snorkel on and jumped into the water.

"We'll see Mr. Scout Leader. Just wait there until my friend is finished," Dimitri said.

Within moments Vitali had retrieved five of the packages and thrown them into the boat. Mike and the Venturers bobbed up and down on the water on their boards. Boris and Vitali trained their handguns on the boys. In Russian, Vitali told Dimitri the total packages recovered so far was six - four to go.

Mike gazed around and saw Mark looking uncomfortable with his feet wrapped tightly around his board. Under the water, Mark was hanging onto one of the packages with his feet and this was becoming increasingly hard to do. Vitali returned with two more packages bringing the total to eight. He paddled behind the sub and dived a couple of times. The ninth package was hard to find as it was wedged in the former outlet of the propeller shaft which had been welded shut but had left a small alcove. Vitali threw the package into the boat and spoke again to Dimitri in Russian saying he couldn't find the last package.

"I will ask you only once Mr Scoutmaster – did you find any of these packages my friend has been retrieving?" Dimitri asked Mike.

"No. If we found anything we would have them in our hands .... we're not carrying any packs. Nor have we been back to the beach," Mike said icily.

Vitali swam towards the boys and dived under. Mark released the package and tried to push it away from himself. Boris noticed it floating to the surface and alerted Dimitri.

"What is this Scoutmaster? A dead fish?" Dimitri asked. "You, in the red shorts ... throw the package into the boat."

The package was floating between Mark and Scott. The younger boy leaned over his board, picked up the package and heaved it into the boat. Vitali surfaced and Dimitri signalled to him to rejoin the boat. In Russian he told him the last package had been found.

Vitali swam to the boat and climbed in. He doffed his fins, mask and snorkel and counted the booty. He then looked at the scene in front of him and realised how serious the situation had become. In Russian, he told Dimitri if he killed the boys and their leader they would never leave Australia and return to Russia. Boris chimed in with how dangerous it was to leave witnesses but was at a loss as to what to do. Dimitri said he could order the group off their boards and make them swim back to the beach. Alternatively, shoot them all and take their chances escaping back to Sydney.

During the heated exchange between the Russians Mike whispered to Peter that the gangsters were arguing about what to do with them. He spoke loudly to all the Venturers and told them to stay calm and do as they were told. All would be fine. Dimitri cocked his weapon and waved it in the air as he spoke animatedly with his team. Finally, Vitali came up with a plan.

"Dimitri, let's tow them to the abandoned lighthouse and lock them inside," Vitali said. "By the time anyone finds them they'll either be dead or we'll be halfway back to Moscow. Either way, we win!"

Dimitri pondered the suggestion for a few moments and agreed. He looked at Mike and told him to paddle closer to the boat.

"My friend here likes you. You are lucky. I want you as fish food. If you don't do as I say now, all of you will be shark bait, with you first," Dimitri said.

"Alright. What do you want us to do?" Mike asked.

"Join all your boards together and tie them to a rope my friend will throw to you."

"Where are you taking us? Some of these boys can't swim too far and will surely die if you take us out to sea and dump us. You don't want that on your hands," Mike said.

Dimitri eyed Mike closely and told him to issue his order. Mike told the Venturers to tie their boards together and for Mark to join the boards to the boat's tow rope. Boris tied off a rope to a railing and threw the free end to Mark who had his hands in the air to catch it. Within minutes the Russians and Venturers were joined together. Mike told the boys again to stay calm and hang onto their boards. He told them to be brave. Scott thought Mike and the boys should do something to thwart the Russians.

He looked at Mike and telepathically tried to tell him, only the brave dare. Scott swallowed hard and thought about his father. If only he could contact his dad, an army of police would descend on these gangsters and arrest them. The tables would be turned. Some of the younger boys were becoming visibly upset.

Scott and Ian spoke calmly to them and told them to concentrate on hanging on to their boards. They could worry later when they knew what was going to happen to them.

Vitali took up the position behind the wheel and slowly took off to allow the tow rope's slack to take up. The boat groaned as it picked up the weight of the Venturers and started ploughing through the water. Boris and Dimitri watched the Venturers from the aft of the boat. They agreed to kill the boys and their leader at the lighthouse if they couldn't lock them away. Both agreed the drug money was too high a price to pay to be caught.

In any case, they would serve a double sentence in an Australian jail. First, they would be serving the sentence imposed on them from the courts. The second would be their execution by hired inmates with contacts to the Russian mafia. Both Dimitri and Boris knew there was no way Moscow would allow them to live and so possibly spoil the lucrative drug trade between Russia and Australia.

Mark and Peter were joined to Mike and discussed whether they should jump the men and take their weapons and inform the police. Mike told them not to even think of it. He said just one Venturer's death would be too high a price for foolishness, never mind any more. Besides, no one knew where they were being towed.

Vitali steered the boat across the bay and out into the open sea. A feeling of controlled panic set in among Mike and the boys when the boat cleared the heads surrounding the bay. The swell wasn't too large so they were not buffeted by large waves as they were towed. The lighthouse came into view and the boat shifted its bearing towards it.

"Thank God they're not taking us out to sea," Mike said out loud.

"Where do you think they'll tow us?" Mark asked.

"My guess is the lighthouse. It's the only secluded area around here with buildings. If that's the case, follow my lead." Mike told the Ventures to be compliant and obey whatever they were ordered to do. However, if the chance came up, he would try and make a move to overpower the men.

Vitali drove his flotilla past the lighthouse and ensured no one could be seen there. He then called to Dimitri and told him all looked clear and that he was going in. The speedboat pulled up to a jetty and Boris tied off a rope to a halyard to secure the vessel. Vitali had already jumped onto the wharf and had started making his way to the caretaker's cottage. Dimitri ordered the boys off their boards and told them to group together on the jetty.

He motioned to Scott to go to him. Scott looked at Mike. His leader acquiesced and nodded for him to join the Russian. When Scott went to Dimitri the Russian put his handgun to the boy's head. Mike flinched and wanted to try and take the gangster.

"Don't make any silly moves Mr Scoutmaster or I will start killing the boys one by one – starting with this one. At this range I can't miss. Think about the boys. They are no match for our weapons."

Mike stiffened and stared icily at the two men. He was the boy's protector on this camp but there was nothing he could do at this moment.

"We'll do as you want. Just don't hurt anyone," Mike said.

"That's better Mr Scoutmaster. Just wait. My friend is trying to arrange a rest area for you," Dimitri said.

Mike could see the picture. He could also see Scott being held by this Russian gangster. Emotions boiled inside Mike but he had no choice but to comply as the boys' lives were at risk. Scott was also in danger of having his brains blown out by this madman. Scott looked at Mike but resisted making any move as he knew the Russian had a firm grip on his shoulder. Scott's mind was racing as he looked for ways to try and turn the tables.

Vitali returned from his investigation of the area. In Russian he told Dimitri that he and Boris could open the main door leading to the old prison cells. Dimitri agreed and his grip on Scott became even harder. Vitali and Boris made their way to a large, wooden and steel gate at the entrance to the sandstone prison. A large chain and brass padlock was wound around two small hand hold openings in the gate. Vitali used his handgun to shoot the lock open.

Boris hardly flinched. He had seen Vitali use his weapon before. Vitali pulled the chain through the gate and opened up. He walked through into an open space area that had offices either side. A large grille gate led into the cell complex. A number of the cells were open as they were in the process of being restored by the government so the whole complex would become a tourist attraction managed by the National Parks and Wildlife Service.

Vitali and Boris made their way back to Dimitri and the Venturers. In Russian, Vitali explained what he had just done and how the cells were open.

"Mr Scoutmaster, this is your lucky day. My offsiders have found a nice, comfortable place for you and the boys. Tell them to get their boards and take them into the prison grounds. Now!"

Mike wasted no time. The Russian gangster still had hold of Scott. Mike knew he could not overpower three armed men – nor could the Venturers. He told the boys to get their boards and take them up to the prison. So far the boys seemed to be holding up alright. Mike was worried about Scott. The boy was only young; he had hardly any life experience and was usually timid or shy around new people. However Mike also knew Scott had the smarts about him and would make the most of any adverse situation.

"We've got all the boards. Let the boy go. He can't harm you," Mike told Dimitri.

"Not so fast Mr Scoutmaster. I may have other uses for him," came the sinister reply.

Dimitri put his left hand onto the collar of Scott's rash shirt and waved his pistol in his right hand to motion for Mike and the boys to go through the gates. Once through, Dimitri told Mike to put all the boards into one of the offices.

While this was happening Vitali kept a watch on the outside approach to the convict prison in case any police or workmen turned up. Boris walked ahead of the boys and opened two cell doors. He motioned for the boys to go inside. Mike told the boys they had no choice and to do as they were told. Again he confronted Dimitri and asked for Scott to be allowed to join his mates.

"No. Not yet. He will go elsewhere and be my insurance. If you try and break out of here and somehow contact the authorities, the boy will be shark meat. Do you understand?"

Fury welled up inside Mike and he took a step forward to press home his point. Dimitri brought his pistol close to Scott's temple.

"If I have to show you that I will kill this boy and then another, and another, to get what I want, then I will do it. Do you want this boy's blood on your hands? If you do, take another step forward and you can catch his brains as I blow them out."

Mike was shocked by the threat and quickly retreated a few steps.

"That's better. This is not a time to be a hero. Co-operate and you live another day. Try to be a hero, and you will all surely die today," Dimitri said. "Now get in there with your boys."

Mike walked into the cell and Boris closed the full metal door and slid the bolt across. He did the same with the second cell that contained the rest of the boys. Scott was now becoming terrified. Dimitri spoke in Russian and asked Boris to scout the place further and see where they could stow Scott.

"Don't worry. Do as you are told and all will be well," Dimitri told the boy. He relaxed the pressure on the rear of Scott's rash shirt and then released him.

Scott's mind was working overtime. If he made a run for it, he would be shot by this gangster. If he tried to overpower the man there was every likelihood Scott would be the one injured. He decided to go along and see what happened. Boris entered the cell passageway from a set of winding stairs.

"Dimitri, halfway up the stairs is the old lighthouse and a spare cell," Boris said in Russian. "The cell must have been for the prisoners that were bad and had to be kept separate."

"Da," Dimitri replied in Russian. "Up you go. My friend has found a room with a view."

Scott started walking to the stairs. He looked behind at Dimitri and asked why he was singled out.

"I want some insurance from your Scoutmaster. If you don't do anything silly, you'll be released from here shortly. Enough talk. Keep moving."

The stairs seemed to wind up the tower forever. Finally, Scott saw Boris holding a cell door open.

The passageway was narrow and every noise echoed around the sandstone walls and ceiling that spiraled upwards for five storeys. The trio came to a landing under the level that contained the electric motors and final gear shaft that operated the giant 250 watt Multi-vapor lamps. Boris waved to Scott to go into the cell. Scott walked into the cell and turned around only to see the thick steel door closing behind him. He flinched when he heard Boris slide the door's bolt into position and a padlock being closed. He was now a prisoner in a lofty tower around five floors above the ground with the other Venturers and Mike below him – somewhere.

Vitali and Boris were halfway down the steep spiraling

staircase when they heard someone running. They stopped when they saw Vitali round a landing.

"Dimitri! A police car is heading this way and there are government boats off the point," Vitali said excitedly in Russian.

"How far away is the police car? Which direction are the government boats heading?" Dimitri asked.

"There is a dirt road that winds through the bush heading towards here from inside the park. The police car is about two kilometres away," Vitali replied excitedly.

"The boats – what sort are they?" Dimitri urged.

"There are two boats heading north but close to here. I think one is Customs and the other a Coastguard vessel."

Dimitri looked at both his men and saw the burgeoning fear on their faces. The last thing he wanted now was a Beslan-type school disaster and stand-off between them and the Australian armed forces.

"Boris, I suggest you take the boat down to the creek, just west of here, cover it and rejoin us," Dimitri ordered. "If we meet the cops, we'll say we're cleaners. We'll look after the love packages in case there are any complications."

Boris quickly ran down to the jetty and started the boat. He drove it a few hundred metres away to where a creek flowed into the bay and slowly made his way into a shaded area. The boat ambled slowly along the creek and suddenly stopped dead in its tracks. Boris was thrown head first into the craft's steering wheel, splitting his forehead open in the process and banging his nose on the centre hub of the wheel. This caused a steady flow of blood to start ensuing from his nostrils. The propeller was stuck fast, entangled in crayfish netting. Boris regained his senses but had a stream of blood oozing down his face.

The head cut was not bad, but ordinarily would have required three or four stitches. The nosebleed was nothing but a nuisance as it allowed blood to flow freely down his mouth and chin. Boris wiped his face with his hand before reaching into the creek and scooping some water to splash over his nose and chin. He clambered out of the boat and covered it with as many branches as possible. When he was satisfied he had camouflaged the boat well, he started making his way up the creek line. Boris kept a lookout for the authorities as he ran to the creek's confluence and stayed within the tree line.

The police car arrived at the lighthouse with a single officer inside. The policeman checked the caretaker's cottage and found it still locked. Constable Shayne Rugless walked up to the combined convict jail and lighthouse and saw a chain and lock. He went to physically check it when he was distracted by a ship's horn being sounded in the bay. Constable Rugless walked down to the edge of the building. He saw a small, white boat with blue writing on it and gave a hearty wave. Three pairs of eyes followed his every movement. Two handguns were trained on him ready to deliver their copper-tipped projectiles to his head.

He started walking back to his car when he noticed a rubber bung on the ground. Carefully he bent down, picked it up and went to his car. He picked up the radio receiver and then replaced it. This was not a good area for car radio reception. Usually Constable Rugless and the lighthouse keeper would share a coffee. He would use the keeper's ham radio base to call in. However, since the lighthouse was being automated and upgraded by contractors, the lighthouse keeper and his family had gone on a vacation. The contractors had stopped work because of the holidays and weren't due back for another week. Constable Rugless drove his car back along the track.

After a few minutes, Boris made his way stealthily to the gate leading into the prison. He pulled at the chain and it moved freely around the handhold and fell into his hands. He had only shot a link out and moved the chain around earlier so at a glance the unsuspecting eye wouldn't notice the broken chain.

"Stupid cop," Boris muttered. Vitali and Dimitri met him as he passed through the gates.

"Has he gone?" Vitali asked.

"Yes. He went to the gate, saw the chain in place and waved to the Customs people before leaving. That should be the last we see of him," Boris stated.

"What happened to you?" Dimitri asked.

"Damn creek. Something fouled the propeller. The boat stopped too quickly and I hit my forehead and nose on the steering wheel," Boris replied.

"Well you had better get cleaned up so you don't drip blood anywhere. The last thing we need is something that will cause a major problem," Vitali said.

"There's a faucet around the corner here. I'll help you. Come on."

The two men walked to the side of the building away from view of the bay. Dimitri instructed Boris to lean his head forward and pinch his own nose. He then turned on the faucet and kept scooping water to wash away the blood on Boris's head. Dimitri checked the gash to ensure there was no major problem. The blood flow finally eased from Boris's nose and head. The pair cleaned up and made their way back to the prison entrance where Vitali was waiting.

"That's a nasty gash. The lighthouse keeper should have some form of first aid kit," Vitali said. "Let's get a cover for it."

"Da," Boris said as Dimitri helped him walk to the lighthouse keeper's hut.

Vitali arrived at the house first. He carefully checked the windows and doors. He was disappointed. A security system had been recently installed.

"Boris, you may have to go without," Vitali said. "The windows and doors look like they have recently been wired up. Probably with some back-to-base type of reporting."

"How do you know this?" Boris asked.

"There are electrical wire endings on the floor inside and outside near the doors. The outside alarm box is near the ceiling in the alcove closest to the front door. Do you want me to go on?"

"No. That's fine."

Vitali looked at his comrades-in-arms. "I think we need to get our heads together and gather our thoughts. Let's go into the jail out of sight and plan our next move," he said.

"Okay. This will give time for the government boats and the local cop to clear out of here."

The three Russians made their way back into the convict prison. They went to the office where the boys had stored their boards and started their planning.

Constable Rugless drove back along the lighthouse road and called in at the home of the local school principal, John Winter. The two had been friends for years with both their sons in different boarding schools. Constable Rugless had turned on his car radio but still could not receive any messages from his police station so he turned it off so he wouldn't continuously hear the hissing and crackling of the device. The two men enjoyed a good coffee and discussion.

CHAPTER TWENTY-THREE

At Customs House in Sydney, Superintendent Clive Hartcher went over the plans once more. The Australian Navy would intercept the Pushkin possibly somewhere near the New South Wales and Queensland State borders. Members of the Special Air Service Regiment would board the vessel and overpower the crew, Customs personnel would then help take it back to Sydney. The Navy crew would 'look after' the Russian sailors. His thoughts were disturbed by the phone.

"Clive, this is Dave Farrell. I just want to update you with Operation Stella."

"Dave, that would be great, thanks. I don't want to talk to Canberra half-cocked with the information I have," Clive Hartcher replied.

"Apparently the State police are proving to be a problem because of communications in the area. They sent a local car out to check the coastline near Myall Lakes and the lighthouse but haven't heard back from him. There's some sort of radio reception problem in the area."

"What about the Navy and the SASR? Are they still on track for an interception this afternoon or tonight?"

"Navy says it has a frigate steaming towards the area but best estimate is that it won't be in position until sometime late tonight. That gives the SASR boys a bit of breathing space and allows them to fly up to the mid-north coast area and use that as a launching area. Once I know what the State boys have found I'll let you know."

"Dave, Customs can give me an armed patrol boat which we can have in the area by tomorrow morning ... maybe late tonight if the seas aren't too rough. The ship can marry up with the Navy frigate and assist where required."

Inspector Farrell again said he would check with the State police and get back to Customs. The pair rang off. The Duty Inspector at Taree police station, Mike Hannan was becoming concerned. He had not heard back from Constable Shayne Rugless. He knew there was a radio black spot in the area near the lighthouse. However, he still liked Constable Rugless to radio in when he reached the main highway and give updates of his patrols. This ensured all was well.

"Boss, we have Inspector Farrell from the Feds back on line for you. Will you take it in your office?" Constable Marie Schaeffer asked.

"Yes please. Put him through to my office." Inspector Hannan walked back to his office from the tea room and picked up the phone.

"Dave, good to hear from you. What's happening?" Inspector Hannan asked.

"Mike, this is a personal call from one friend to another. You'll be briefed further by your own Assistant Commissioner shortly. However, there is a major operation underway to catch a Russian ship. It appears it may have dropped off some drugs somewhere in your patrol area."

Mike Hannan thought for a moment. This was turning out to be a bigger day than he had envisaged.

"What sort of ship and what sort of drugs? I mean, where were they dropped off and who is involved?"

"Mike, Navy, the Army and Customs are all involved. Apparently a Russian trawler dropped off some drugs or other contraband in your area last night. The ship has been closely monitored by the Navy and is to be intercepted later. In the meantime, keep a close eye on anything suspicious in your patrol area," Inspector Farrell advised.

"Dave thanks for that. So far all has been quiet. However, I still have patrols out and they haven't reported in as yet. Please keep me in the loop; it saves surprises from the top."

"No problems Mike, I'll be in touch."

The two rang off and Mike Hannan called his senior sergeant into his office. He briefed the sergeant to ensure all the police on patrol reported any suspicious behaviour or problems in the community, regardless of how insignificant it may appear.

CHAPTER TWENTY-FOUR

Scott looked around his cell. It was like being in a broom closet. It became instantly obvious the gangsters had only opened the door and peered in. If they had entered the cell they would have discovered the workmen's gear behind the door. He took a moment to go through the equipment and see what was of any use to him. Next, Scott took a metal bucket from behind the door and placed it under the window cell. The window was a small opening with two metal bars set horizontally. It was also just out of reach of Scott.

The window had no glass and would have let the rain in upon the convicts who originally occupied the cell. For now, it was letting in light and lots of fresh air. Scott checked the workmen's gear and found a small length of rope and piece of water pipe. The two items would make a great tool for Scott but he still couldn't reach the window to see out. He knew if he attached the pipe to the rope and tried to throw it through the window opening, the resulting noise could bring him grief from the gangsters. He stopped and tried to think through his problem. Scott looked more closely at his cell. It was constructed to accommodate up to three or four men in hammocks tied to bolts in the walls. His plan was quick to come into play. He wrapped the end of the rope around his right wrist and stood on the upturned bucket. Scott then stepped onto a lower metal lug that was designed for a bottom hammock and was set into the wall.

He pushed himself upright against the wall and tried to balance on the lug. Scott reached for the bars but was still too short. He looked up and saw another lug offset in the wall for the top hammock. Scott reached for the lug and fell. After dusting off himself, and his pride, he climbed back on top of the first lug. He then pulled the rope up from his wrist and threw it up to the bars. The end looped around the top bar and trailed against the sill.

Scott stood his full height on the lug and grabbed the end of the rope. He quickly tied a bowline in the free end of the rope and fed the rest through the open loop. The youth pulled on the rope and it tightened upon itself, providing him with a useful anchorage and climbing tool. Now he could pull on the rope and stand on the top lug to look out.

The view out the window was beautiful and scary. It was beautiful because it allowed Scott to see the waves rolling in and crashing onto the nearby beach. It was also scary as it showed Scott how high up he was – taller than some of the large trees he had seen on the way to the lighthouse. He grabbed the rope and climbed onto the window sill area to see what was outside his cell. A notion of bravado ran through him as he pondered escape.

Problem one: it was too far to the ground with only a short rope, if he fitted through the bars. Problem two: if he managed to get outside his window, could he climb up to the actual lighthouse area? He pulled tightly upon the rope as he squashed his body further into the sill area. He tried to push his face between the bars when the top one started giving way. The sudden loosening of the bar overbalanced Scott, forcing him to fall to the ground with the iron bar in tow. The impact knocked the wind out of Scott and the iron bar hit his head, knocking him unconscious.

"Sshh! Did you hear that?" Vitali asked. The other two men stopped what they were doing and craned their necks. Vitali walked towards a window and looked out from the side.

"There is nothing outside ... maybe it was the boys getting restless?" he suggested.

Vitali looked at him and said they should do a reconnaissance of the area in another few minutes. He was anxious to get back into the boat and return to the wharf and pick up the group's car and escape to Sydney.

Vitali wanted to be somewhere else. Anywhere, except at the lighthouse, as it was a dead end area with nowhere to retreat. Boris said he would help to get the boat running again. Both Boris and Dimitri made their way out of the lighthouse jail area. They readjusted the chain around the entrance gate, made sure no one was around and made their way into the thick bushland. The pair negotiated the scrub and heavy bush to where Boris had left the boat covered with bracken and ferns.

"The boat was well hidden ... I don't think anyone could have found it from the water," Dimitri said.

"Coming from you comrade, that is a compliment. We'll have to check out the propeller to see what snared it," Boris said.

The two Russians set to work to expose the boat and move the cover from the top. It didn't take long. The sleek hire boat was soon visible again.

"Boris, check out the propeller while I check the engine," Dimitri ordered.

"Da. Don't attempt to turn on the engine until you warn me," Boris cautioned as he reached for the craft's toolbox.

"You worry too much. I'm just going to check the engine housing to ensure all is still relatively well. When you give me the okay signal I will try and start them. Phew!"

Boris waded into the water until he reached the rear of the boat. He stopped, thinking.

"Dimitri, throw me some goggles and a snorkel so I can look at the prop underwater."

"No problems," Dimitri said as he fossicked in the boat for Boris's equipment.

His friend's snorkel and mask were easy to find as they were the only ones made of all-black rubber surrounds. Both Dimitri's and Boris's masks and fins had various coloured surrounds. Boris rinsed his mask in the water, spat in it and spread his saliva over the lens. This was to create a surface tension break and allow him to see without the mask fogging up on the inside. Boris then asked Dimitri to stand next to him while he held his shoulders with one hand and donned his fins with the other. Then, without further ado, Boris took his knife from the scabbard on his leg, held his breath, and slipped beneath the murky water.

Within seconds he found the cause of the problem - netting wound tightly around the prop. Boris sliced into the nylon netting and pulled a handful from the prop before surfacing, taking a gulp of air and diving back down. He did the routine for several minutes before finally signalling to Dimitri that all was well.

Dimitri had cleaned up the bloodied steering wheel and inside the boat. He gestured to Boris to swim clear and he tried to start the boat's engine. The battery had plenty of power but the engine wouldn't kick into life. Dimitri opened the engine cowling and tinkered. Several times he tried to start the engine but to no avail.

Finally he gave up. Boris doffed his mask and fins and clambered into the boat. He tried a number of times to start the engine but had the same response as Dimitri – nothing. Both men called it a day and covered the boat with ferns and branches again before heading back to the lighthouse jail. Vitali had been in the office looking at old records and plans of the jail and lighthouse.

"We have tried many times, but we can't get the engine started," Boris reported. "Maybe the engine seized when the prop fouled?"

He waited for what seemed an eternity for the resultant explosion from Vitali. When it happened – he wasn't disappointed. Vitali seemed to be holding his breath as his eyes began to bulge. His face contorted and went a deep beetroot colour.

"If you want to get out of this god forsaken jail and go home we have to fix that boat! DO YOU HEAR ME?" he yelled at both men. "I have studied the plans for this place and there are only two ways out of here. The road out through the forest and back to the main highway or by sea to where we picked up the boys," Vitali barked. "I don't feel like a swim or a long walk and both could be dangerous with the police and Customs patrolling the area."

Boris studied his boss for a moment. "Maybe if you came back with us your mechanical knowledge might get us out of here," he said.

"What about the boys?" Dimitri asked.

"They're not going anywhere. You could say they are quite secure in their new lodgings," Vitali answered as he started to regain colour in his face.

"Alright. Do we need any other tools or equipment?" Vitali asked.

"No. I don't think this will get us any further, but then again ... you may have the magic touch," Dimitri said as he looked to Boris for support.

Boris picked up on the vibes.

"We've tried everything we can, however, I learnt long ago from you that fresh eyes can often see something tired eyes can't," he said.

An unsaid mutual agreement passed over the three men. Vitali closed his historical book. He looked at the other two men in turn and started to walk out of the office. The other two followed. They made their way out of the main gates and headed to the wooded area and along the waterway to the boat. Vitali helped uncover the vessel and set to work investigating the starter problem.

CHAPTER TWENTY-FIVE

Scott became slowly aware of his surroundings. He had a pounding headache and a bump the size of an egg on the back of his head. He focused, felt his head and face. Nothing damaged. No bleeding.

'Okay Scott, what would Mike do?' the boy asked himself in a muffled tone. 'Well, he wouldn't just lie here - he'd get up and try again.'

Easier thought than done. Even though Scott had good balance he felt unsure and therefore didn't push himself as much. At least on the submarine he was boss of the wash. For some inextricable reason Scott had clambered up the side of the sub amid broiling water and made it on deck. He was then able to assist some of the other Venturers before the Russians arrived. The room stopped spinning. Scott thought about where he was incarcerated and started evaluating his position. It was an old jail with a lighthouse built on top. His cell was near the top of the column that was the lighthouse.

If he managed to get to the window cell and then outside; he could only go up to the housing containing the actual lantern and its magnified prism. Falling down the side of the lighthouse and onto the rocks below was not an option. Scott tried climbing up the bolts on the wall again.

This time he tucked his metal rod and rope down the front of his T-shirt. He clambered confidently from bolt to bolt. The youth put all his weight on his toes and balanced on the tallest lug. He leant against the wall and gingerly pulled out his rod and rope. He gathered the rope in his left hand and fed a small length to his right.

Slowly, Scott twirled the rope and rod and threw it up to the barred window recess. The rod went sailing through the remaining bars along with some rope. Scott jerked back on the rope and the rod pulled hard against the bars, locking tight. He gave a sigh of relief and started to shimmy up the rope and wall to the window sill. The noise was minimal.

Unless the gangsters were right outside his cell door Scott didn't believe they would have heard him. Slowly, he reached up, grabbed the bottom bar, and pulled himself onto the ledge. Scott's breathing was fast and his heart seemed to want to push between his ribs and leave his body. He sat on the ledge holding his rope tight, trying to calm down and control his breathing. Within a few minutes Scott had regained his composure and dared to look out the window.

At first the view was daunting. Broiling surf crashed onto rocks about fifteen metres below. Out to the south east was the national park. Not a house to be seen anywhere. He only had a few metres of rope which was not enough to abseil on. The drop after the rope ran out would be fatal. This was not like the movies with the escapee falling into a deep, calm sea. There were huge, sharp rocks below and surf that didn't want visitors. Scott swallowed hard. Maybe the answer was upwards. His cell was near the top of the lighthouse.

He held tight onto his rope and put his head outside the window. Surely this was suicide to attempt any climb? Then again ... maybe not. The bricks for the lighthouse were not totally flush. The underside of a verandah that went around the whole of the tower was in reach if Scott could make it up the tower wall. The thought of the whole process made Scott tremble.

He knew Mike and the others were in ground floor cells. Hopefully they could launch an escape bid and rescue him. Scott pondered the situation and then made up his mind. Mike would have let him know somehow by now if he could, or had already, escaped. No. The escape plot was

Scott's – solely. There was no back up, any way of letting Mike know what Scott was doing. He just had to try. No, he had to do it – and succeed.

What he was going to do when on top of the verandah – if he made it – he was not sure about. Scott leant his head out the window and looked up. Around two metres up were the wooden under supports for the verandah. They were similar to buttresses in churches – only miniature in comparison. Each of the buttresses jutted out at a forty-five degree angle joining the main wall of the lighthouse to the extended verandah.

Scott thought for a moment. He would have to brace himself in the window and throw the pipe and rope up to the closest buttress. Hopefully, the pipe would fly through the gap between the buttress and wall and lodge in the associated V-shape at its base. This would allow Scott to climb up the rope to the buttress and then ... Scott never finished his train of thought. He was impatient to start and complete the task ahead. He checked the knot around the pipe. Scott mentally measured the distance between himself and the buttress. He thought he would just make it. Quickly he gathered the rope and coiled it.

He picked up the pipe and placed it in his right hand, the rope he left in his left. Scott leant out the window, twirled the pipe in a circle and threw it towards the buttress. The pipe bounced off the buttress and started to fall. Scott pulled in the rope and tried again. This time he threw the pipe like a spear and it flew through the gap of the buttress and wall. There were only a few centimetres of rope left in his hand, and a feeling of joy washed over him as the realisation of his achievement hit home.

"Now all I have to do is swing out from the window shelf, climb out of the cell and up the rope," Scott said to himself. He looked down and felt queasy. It was a long drop from which there was no return. Scott was no hero, he just had a job to do – to help save his fellow Venturers. Slowly, he edged his backside across the window shelf and brought his feet up to his waist.

He pushed his head out of the window and pulled tightly on the rope. Everything seemed to be holding firm. Scott pulled himself out of the window and swung on the rope until it was directly under the buttress. The hard work began. Scott slowly climbed hand over hand up the rope. He was acutely aware that if he fumbled or let go, all his efforts would have been in vain and he would be dead. Sweat started pouring down Scott's forehead.

He was able to find the top edges of the bricks and so, take some of his weight on his toes. A shadow started crossing over him as he reached the base of the buttress. Scott was almost there. The gangly youth reached up and found the wooden base. He stood on the absolute top of his toes and was able to reach a few centimetres higher. The shadow of the buttress gave way as his hands found the familiar V-shape of the joint. One last pull upwards and he as able to start reaching through the joint. Like a cat climbing a high surface, Scott scratched at the wall with his feet as he pulled himself upwards into the joint.

The climb had been quite strenuous, so Scott rested by laying within the joint for a few minutes. He knew in time to come when he could look back at this moment he would laugh. After all, this was the first time he had ever been relaxed by a joint - and he wasn't even smoking it! Scott had draped himself over the joint like a leopard up a tree.

It was time to move again and finish the climb. Looking up, Scott saw the underside of the verandah that made its way around the whole of the lighthouse. The base of the verandah rested on a series of joints spread evenly around the outer top of the lighthouse. Slowly, he inched his way to the top of the joint and jammed his feet into the bottom V-shape for leverage.

Scott did not look down. He knew if he did he would feel very scared and then not be able to complete the climb. Scott reached over the verandah for a railing post and found one. He then lay back on the buttress and pulled up the rope and grabbed the pipe. The climbing gear was pushed down the front of his shirt. Scott rested. The whole activity had been very draining. He hung on tightly to the buttress with his knees and hand.

'Okay Scott. This is the last part. You can do it!' Scott thought to himself. 'One last manoeuvre and we're safe again.' Scott eased himself up along the buttress and reached for the verandah. He did a combined movement of sliding forwards and reaching over the verandah and gripping the rail post. An inner strength flowed through the youth as he put his head over the verandah slats and swung his legs up onto the wooden footway. A few seconds later, and Scott was able to roll on the verandah next to the wall. He closed his eyes and cried as emotion took over as a form of relief from tension. Somewhere down below were Mike and the Venturers.

He hoped his action of escaping did not jeopardise anyone, however the cost of escaping and maybe alerting authorities to the presence of the gangsters may save some lives. Tears of satisfaction flowed as he realised he had just done something he would have thought impossible some months ago. However, ever since Scott had joined the Venturers, his confidence in himself had been boosted by Mike.

The Venturers had also encouraged him to push himself that little bit further each time - to go beyond the comfort zone. So far he had passed the test. Now to work out what to do from here onwards.

CHAPTER TWENTY-SIX

"Dimitri, start the engine," Vitali ordered.

A mechanical splutter filled the air as the engine tried to start. Boris looked at Dimitri and raised his eyebrows. Vitali didn't see the men exchange looks. He was too busy tinkering with engine leads and spark plugs.

"Dimitri, again please," Vitali said.

The boat sounded like an overheated lawnmower trying to start.

"I think we have some work to do here," Dimitri said.

"Boris, pass the toolbox. Let's see what this baby is hiding," Vitali said.

While Vitali and Boris worked on the engine, Dimitri kept a watch for any unwanted visitors.

Sergeant Tim Sullivan was called into Inspector Hannan's office.

"Any word from Rugless yet?"

"Not yet boss."

The Inspector shuffled some papers on his desk.

"I am starting to get too many federal agency calls about these Russians. Track him down and get him to contact me. I need local on-the-ground information," Inspector Hannan said.

"Will do. I think he has stopped off somewhere for a coffee as he usually does. Whatever, I'll start the ring around." Sergeant Sullivan returned to his own office. 'Damn that Rugless ... where is he?' he said to himself.

He pulled out his address book and started leafing through it. Constable Rugless was a good cop. He was not one to be out shirking his duties. Sergeant Sullivan knew Constable Rugless would be out doing his job – wherever he was – and gathering information about his patrol area. Rugless was more than capable of becoming a commissioned officer in time to come. He started making his calls.

Admiral Ritchie had become anxious. The Prime Minister's office had been in contact to find out what the situation was in relation to the Russians. Exactly how long before the Navy could intercept the Russian freighter and the Special Air Service Regiment took control of the vessel was still up in the air – literally.

The special Australian Defence satellite covering the region where the freighter was currently steaming through was having transmission difficulties. The Australian Defence Signals Directorate based in Canberra had sought satellite assistance from Washington. The United States have a series of satellites in the south east region as part of their global footprint. An official request from Canberra to Washington was sent via defence channels, and an American 'bird' was programmed to help cover the Australian naval action. The problem was, the satellite would not be in the right global position for a few hours.

At Customs there was a lull in operations too. The Australian Customs vessel, Lady Yvonne was still a few hours from sighting the Australian Navy frigate ship HMAS Eastralia and linking up.

CHAPTER TWENTY-SEVEN

Scott knelt and slowly lifted his body to allow him to peer into the room housing the giant lantern and its huge magnifying lenses that cast its beam for kilometres out to sea. No one was in the room. The lantern stood on a huge, rotating base in the centre of the room. Stairs led to a room below the lantern and a door opened onto the verandah where Scott knelt. Scott raised himself up onto his feet and then squatted. He waddled like a duck round the verandah so his head could not be seen above the window sill until he reached the door.

Slowly, Scott surveyed the inside of the lantern room. He then waddled across to the railing to see if he could see any of the Russians outside in the grounds of the lighthouse jail. Satisfied no one could see him; Scott made his way to the door. He turned the knob – but the door was locked. A grimace came over the teenager's face.

"Too bad. I have no choice," Scott said to himself.

He took off the rash shirt he used to stave off sunburn in the hot Australian sun. Scott wound the shirt round his hand. He quickly punched a small pane of glass above the door handle sending a small shower of glass shards to the floor inside. Scott put his ear to the opening he had just made and strained to hear whether his captors had responded to the noise.

He heard nothing and so put his hand through the open pane and pulled back a bolt lock. Scott turned the door handle which released a recessed button lock and he was able to open the door. Quietly, the youth entered the lantern chamber. Scott's mind went into overdrive.

'Could he slip down the stairs quietly and free Mike and the Venturers? Or should he try and set the lantern in motion and alert passing fisherman to his plight?' The first part of his question was answered quickly. Scott looked down and saw a trapdoor. It had a deadlock on it so intruders couldn't exit the door unless they had a key. Scott turned his attention to the lantern mechanism.

The lantern itself was like the bulb of a giant tulip. The lamp and its magnified lenses were the flower's bulb while the main power lines to the base of the lantern were the body. The lantern was also an island. It stood atop an unseen base that had a circular floor around it and window panels, a door and an exterior verandah or gallery. The control panels were under the floor Scott was standing on. He used a small ladder to climb down to the base of the lantern and into the control room. Scott checked the trapdoor to confirm it was locked – it was.

He investigated around the panels and benches in case a spare key had been left for the keeper. There was none. No telephone was in the control room. Scott thought his luck had changed when he saw an intercom module. He dare not push any buttons in case this alerted the Russians to his presence. There were a series of buttons on the panel.

In the centre of the room stood the lantern that housed the lamp used to alert shipping to coastal dangers. Scott ran his eyes over the apparatus. A series of giant magnified lenses covered the lamps in a circular fashion.

A large spindle turned the lantern. Motors and electrics for the lantern were housed on the lower level where technicians could adjust the apparatus as required. Scott climbed his way down to the lower level to have a closer look. Electric motors were bolted on racks to drive the gear shaft which turned the lantern. Scott was amazed at all the power leads and motors, panels and switches that had replaced the lighthouse keeper.

Four rows of huge batteries stood silent guard to the lamp changer and a computer system had been built to ensure the lamps burnt continuously on a daily basis. Scott checked the panels in case he could use anything. The rows of buttons and meters were confusing.

He checked the inside of the panel doors for instruction manuals. His dad used to keep instruction books near appliances back at home. The practice used to drive Scott's mother mad. She believed the manuals made the home untidy and should have been kept in a central place. Scott's father believed the books should be easily accessible in the event the appliances broke down – as they invariably did. His dad won the day.

When Scott opened the second panel box, a technician's guide fell out. Providence! Scott glanced at the guide and then the panel box, but nothing made sense. He replaced the book and went to the trapdoor that led downstairs to his former cell and those of Mike and the other Venturers. The door would not budge.

'Well, here I am in the top of the lighthouse with no way of escape,' Scott said to himself. 'There has to be something I can do to either escape or alert someone to what is happening.' He sat down and started thinking of what he could do.

"Peter, how are the bars?" Mike asked.

"Extremely tight," Peter replied as he pulled heavily on the bars across their cell window. "These have really been made to stay put. What about the door?"

Mike had checked all the way around the black painted, heavy steel door. The hinges were on the outside. A small flap or peephole was in the centre of the door about two thirds of the way up, it was able to be opened from the corridor. Prison guards used to pull down the flap to check on the inmates while doing their rounds.

"I can only see a small way down the corridor each way," Mike said. "I can't see any Russians – or Scott. Maybe it's time to check on our captors."

Mike cupped his hands to his face and took a deep breath.

"Hey! Anyone home? We need some water!" he yelled.

Mike's voice resonated down the corridor. Venturers in the adjoining cell took up the same catch cry.

"Hey, anyone home? We need some water!" The problem was, the voices echoed along the corridor and distorted the words each person was yelling.

Scott sat bolt upright when he heard Mike's voice. He was about to add to the chorus when reason chimed in. 'What if the Russians were looking for him?'

He didn't want to give his position away. After all, he was in the prime seat. Also, there was nowhere to hide. The only escape would be off the verandah and over the side to the rocks and water below. A thought came to Scott and he went back to the cabinet with the guide book.

CHAPTER TWENTY-EIGHT

The Principal's phone rang and interrupted the two men talking.

"Dad, it's for Constable Rugless," John Winter's youngest son Ross announced.

Constable Rugless picked up the handset.

"Hello, this is Constable Rugless."

"Shayne, this is Sergeant Sullivan, I've been trying for some time to reach you on your radio and mobile phone. Are you okay?"

"Yes Sarge, apologies for not being in better contact, but there is no radio or mobile phone coverage here."

"Shayne, we have reports of some Russian drug runners possibly in the area, so be on the lookout."

He then briefed his young officer on what was happening.

"I've been to the old lighthouse and it seems intact. The gates were locked and no one was around," Constable Rugless told his superior. "However, when I was checking the main gate I found a surfboard bung."

"That's interesting. We think a party of Scouts is missing or perhaps just out for the day. They're camped at Mungo Brush and their bus and trailer were found on the beach a short while ago. If you see them, issue them with a warning about parking on the beach. Check in every thirty minutes for any updates on the Russians."

"Okay boss," Constable Rugless hung up the phone. He looked at the principal.

"We may have some action around here in the next few days."

"Why is that?" the principal asked.

"We have had reports some Russians may be in the area. They apparently retrieved some drugs dropped off by a freighter."

"Shayne, there is nowhere here where a freighter could berth. It would have to use some sort of smaller boat to drop their cargo off in a cove, on a beach or ..."

The two men followed the logic together and in unison said, "... on a partly submerged submarine!"

Both men laughed when they heard each other complete the sentence.

"I am beginning to get a weird feeling about this. It may be nothing, but a short while ago some surfers reported a bus and trailer belonging to a party of Scouts on the beach near where the submarine is situated," Constable Rugless said.

"You don't suspect a group of organised teenage boy Scouts are involved in drug running?" Winters asked.

"No, of course not! But there may be a connection. I just have a weird feeling about this."

Constable Rugless then said his goodbyes and got back into his police car and drove off. He headed towards the highway. During the drive the conversation with his sergeant played over and over in his mind. Constable Rugless decided to check out the bus and trailer left on the beach. At least here were tangible pieces of evidence he could see.

Inspector Dave Farrell was a thorough man. The Australian Federal Police had taught him well. Even though he was a pretty logical person, it was the Feds that had helped him to look after the small detail and so enable him to draw a better big picture when trying to solve cases. He thought about

Myall Lakes again and felt there were loose ends. A number of other times when he felt like this, he would start mind-mapping the information he had. There was no order, just pieces of information drawn into circles with lines connecting them like cartoon dumbbells.

Over the next twenty minutes, Inspector Farrell drew on a giant presentation whiteboard. He picked up his cup from his desk and went and made a cup of tea in the staff kitchen. A few minutes later he was back at his desk surveying his handiwork. He checked his notes and operational updates. The first thing he identified as missing was the Russians who rented a small boat, that is, if they were in fact Russians. Farrell picked up the phone and rang his New South Wales State police counterparts.

'The State police had no idea where the Russian trawler was – check.'

'Defence would know through their satellite imagery – check.'

'No sight of the men who hired the small boat earlier – check.'

'The local policeman at Myall Lakes had radioed in – check.'

'A small bus belonging to a Venturer unit found abandoned on the beach. No connection. Keep.'

'Possible drop-off point for the Russian trawler would be the former Royal Australian Navy submarine floundering off the beach near Myall Lakes – needs further checking with Defence.'

'Await further updates from the local police.'

Admiral Ritchie was not as logical as Inspector Farrell. He had interviewed Submarine Commander Jeff Potter at length as to where someone could possibly hide any packages of drugs on a partly-submerged submarine. The admiral wanted straight, finite answers - nothing esoteric. The information was passed on to the Federal police. In short, there were lots of places small packages could have been placed in and around the sealed submarine.

The American defence satellite was about to come on line and hopefully pinpoint exactly where the Russian trawler was ... he hoped. The 'bird' would assist analysts to gauge what heading the ship would take and how long for one of his ships, and Customs, to intercept her.

A section of the Special Air Service Regiment had already flown north from Sydney in Black Hawk helicopters to take them to HMAS Eastralia heading towards the Russian trawler's last known position.

CHAPTER TWENTY-NINE

Dimitri worked hard to get the boat's engine started, but to no avail. A couple of times the engine sputtered into life, only to stop again amidst a plume of smoke.

"What if we rang the boat hire place and asked them to send a replacement," Vitali suggested.

Dimitri looked directly at him. "Ordinarily, that would be a good suggestion," Dimitri said. "The problem now is we may have the Coast Guard and police looking for us."

"What about the boys?" Boris asked.

"Precisely why we have to fix this boat ourselves and get out of here. The boys will be our guarantee of freedom if all turns to crap," Dimitri said. "Do you want me to go back and check on them to ensure all is well?"

"Da. At least we'll know our second precious cargo is fine," Dimitri said as he reached for another spanner.

Boris walked off but only got fifty metres before Dimitri called him back.

"Comrade, sorry about this, but I think if we pull the engine off the boat we'll have a better chance of fixing it. In any case, the boys aren't going anywhere and no one can hear them."

Boris looked at Vitali and then at Dimitri and nodded.

"It will take the three of us to lift and carry the engine over to the bank," Dimitri said as he wiped some sweat from his brow. "Hopefully it won't take long now."

The three men were becoming resigned to the fact their adventure was getting riskier every minute. They had ten kilograms of drugs worth possibly millions of dollars and a gaggle of teenage boys plus their leader locked up in a convict-built jail. The escape routes were either land or sea. Air was not a possibility, as helicopters had not figured in their escape plan. Both exit points were a problem in terms of escaping unnoticed. The best thing to do was to fix the boat, ditch it somewhere close to where their car was, and drive into the teeming traffic and anonymity.

Scott's investigation seemed to have paid off. He checked the guide book again and opened each of the control panels until he found one that matched his book. The phrasing and diagrams were gobbledygook to him, but he persevered. Somehow, he could use this situation to his advantage.

He had to ensure his captors could not find him and also that the outside world was alerted to the fact he was being held captive. Scott checked every nook and cranny in the top of the lighthouse. In the drawer of a desk, he found a pair of scissors, a pen, some sticky tape and other office stationery. He sat back on the floor and wondered about his predicament. Anytime now he could smash the globes, the huge magnifying lenses or the machinery.

The non-activity of the lighthouse would certainly attract attention. But how would this affect Mike and the other Venturers? The non-activity would only be noticed at night when the lighthouse usually operated. Was there anything else Scott could do to attract attention? The teenager climbed back up to the verandah door. He quickly opened it and slid outside once more onto the verandah. Scott crouched slowly to his knees and peered over the railing.

'What a great day for a swim,' he thought. 'It's warm; seas are slight and not a cloud in the sky. Pity about being in jail.'

He gazed around as much as possible. No one was in sight. No sounds were emanating from the cells below. This was eerie. He slowly slid back inside the lantern room and made his way to the trapdoor. It was definitely locked from both sides. In one sense, it was good the door was locked, as it meant he would be forewarned if the Russians came looking for him. On the other hand, it kept him as trapped as his fellow Venturers below - except he had more freedom to move around, and a better view. He sat down and looked at the giant globe at the base of the magnifying lenses. An idea came to mind and he got busy in his 'office'.

"Mike, it can't be done," Mark said as he pulled on the cell window bars. "These were obviously built too strong just to pull out."

"Okay. Come on down and let's re-think this, there has to be a way out," Mike said.

"If there was Mike, the original prisoners in this jail would have thought about it and escaped," Peter chimed in.

"They may not have wanted to escape," Mark said as his feet hit the floor. "When this lighthouse was built, there was nothing to support life as the convicts knew it outside these walls."

Mike read the concerned faces of his Venturers.

"They only had the wild bush and Aborigines to contend with, no armed and dangerous mad Russians. What I was trying to say before was that with our modern thinking is there any way we can escape? We have modern smarts and we have all grown up with TV where we have seen people break out of jail," Mike continued.

Ian looked at Mike and then played with his toes as he sat on the floor. Without looking up he said loudly, "If you think about it, the only type of jails people broke out of in movies were American. They have open-grilled cells. These jails were built to the British system, and not many people escaped from their jails - especially in the colonies."

Mike walked over to Ian and put his hand on his head.

"You are right, but there must be something we can do to escape this menagerie that the poor old laggers from two centuries ago couldn't," he said.

Mike asked the boys to gather around the door. "I've just had an idea and we need to see whether it will work," he said.

The boys looked quizzically at their leader.

"Let's try and lift the door from its hinges! It could mean an easy way out."

Mike and three of the boys leant against the door and pushed their hands hard on the heavy, metal plating.

"On the count of three, try and lift the door. One, two, three!" Mike commanded.

There was no movement at the door. The four tried twice more before giving up.

"I remember a movie where a pirate was jailed and he escaped by leveraging the door off its hinges," Mike lamented. "It was worth a go."

"Mike, any idea to escape from here is a good idea," Peter said.

"We just have to keep trying. After all, it would be our luck the Russians have left and locked up after themselves so no one will know we are here. Therefore, it would be a travesty if we didn't try everything we could to escape."

Peter sat back on the floor and put his head in his hands. Mike walked over to him and put his hand on Peter's head.

"Thanks Peter, we all needed that," Mike said. "I hope Scott has had some luck."

Ian looked up from his corner of the cell. "Let's hope the Russians have no funny designs on Scott and that he is okay," he said.

Mike looked up and saw Mark still hanging onto the cell window. "Mark, yell out to Scott a couple of times to see if he can hear us," he suggested.

Mark cupped his hands and yelled out, "Scott! Are you okay?"

Scott stood up when he heard his name being called. He initially didn't reply from inside the control room just in case the Russians were nearby. Instead, he slinked carefully onto the verandah and yelled out, "Mike! Mike! Can you hear me?"

"Scott! Are you okay?" Mark yelled back.

"Yes!"

"Hang in there! We'll hopefully be out soon!" came Mark's reply.

A small cheer went up in Mike's cell when they faintly heard Scott's voice. At least he was okay, Mike told everyone. Mark yelled to Scott again, but there was no reply.

Scott became worried he would give his position away by constantly yelling and drawing attention to himself. He sat down with his back to the control room and his feet touching the verandah railing. A feeling of comfort swept over him after he heard one of the Venturers' voices call out to him. The sounds had been slightly muffled because of the heavy sandstone bricks that comprised the cell. However, it was great hearing them. Scott couldn't work out exactly from where the sounds emanated, but he had a general idea.

Constable Rugless drove along the meandering dirt road to a hill overlooking the beach. He could see Mike's bus and trailer parked on the apron of the beach, just off the roadway.

A quick scan of the area revealed no one else was around. He drove to the bus site and reported in by radio. The 22-seater bus and trailer were both neatly parked on a sandy strip leading to the entrance of the beach. Constable Rugless peered through the windows and saw a motley collection of towels, jackets and pullovers on the seats and floors. There seemed to be nothing untoward within the bus.

He checked the trailer. The canvas flaps were zippered down and rope cord continuously wound around railings on the lip of the trailer and eyelets at the bottom of the canvas cover. Nothing seemed disturbed. He radioed his boss.

"Yeah Sergeant, its Shayne Rugless. I'm at the abandoned bus and trailer on the beach," he said. "It's all intact. There must be a few kids around somewhere. The bus looks like a mobile change room for a Venturer unit. It has heaps of blue shirts and cream coloured pants uniforms hanging up inside it."

"Shayne, touch nothing. The Feds are on their way and they need to see the bus," Sergeant Sullivan answered.

"Okay."

"Can you see anyone out at the submarine from where you are?"

"No. I checked that as I approached the beach. By the footprints it looks like a gaggle of people have got out of the bus, milled around the trailer and then gone for a swim."

"You may want to check out the next headland in case you can see the boys."

"Alright Sergeant. Back to you soon."

Constable Rugless replaced the radio in its cradle and drove to a headland north of Mungo Brush. Using large, police-issued binoculars he scoured the sea and surrounds. He could see the sub with waves breaking over it. He could see the beach escarpment. Nowhere could he see the Venturers, their boards or their leader. There were not many places you could go for a swim and not be seen on the surrounding coastline.

Constable Rugless put his right hand into his pocket and felt the piece of bung cord. He pulled it out of his pocket and picked up the radio transmitter. This time Sergeant Sullivan was quick to respond.

"Sergeant there's no one in sight along the coast," he told his boss. "A Scout group with colourful boards just doesn't disappear off the coastline. They would have to have gone somewhere else."

"Shayne in about an hour's time the beach you're on now and the submarine will be crawling with Federal cops and military personnel," Sergeant Sullivan said.

"Do you want me to check out the old jail once more in case the Venturers have been taken there?" Constable Rugless asked.

"No, not yet. I'll need you to assist the Feds. Anyhow, you would need a pretty big boat to put all the kids' boards into and take them away. I've lived in this area for more than fifteen years and I can't think of any locals with a boat that big.

"Then you'd have to ask why they would want so many teenagers as hostages. Hell, I have two teenage boys and they're a handful, never mind twenty or so of the buggers," Sergeant Sullivan said.

"Alright Sergeant, I'll wait here for the Feds to arrive," Constable Rugless replied.

Constable Rugless was caught between a rock and a hard place. On the one hand he had to babysit an empty bus and trailer. On the other there was a notion that somehow the Venturers had suffered some form of misadventure. The old jail could still prove to be the key to the riddle.

CHAPTER THIRTY

Dimitri was worried. He had a lot riding on these packages from the motherland. The last thing he needed was a major mess where no one won.

"Vitali! Check the boat for any water repellent-type spray. It just may work," Dimitri demanded.

"Da. If this does not get us going we will need to rethink our options," Vitali replied.

He looked at Boris for support.

"What do you mean comrade?" Dimitri asked.

Vitali steeled himself. "If this boat doesn't start, we will need to get off this peninsula, join the mainstream traffic and get the hell out of here as soon as possible."

Dimitri felt his blood boil. In Russia he probably could have shot Vitali for such insubordination. Instead, he knew he needed both Vitali and Boris to escape as well. His body relaxed a tad.

"You are right. Like you, I just want out of here so we can complete our mission. We have a lot riding on this."

Dimitri smiled. "Will you help us all to escape this Aussie Alcatraz?" he asked.

The two other Russians looked at him and also smiled. Vitali went searching through the boat for water-repellent spray while Boris helped Dimitri to clean and dry the engine. All seemed settled for the moment. The three worked in unison to get the motor repaired.

"Peter, how loose is the bed frame?" Mike asked.

Peter looked at his Venturer leader quizzically before the penny dropped. He started feeling the frame to see whether it could be broken. Maybe it could be used for their escape? Both tugged and pulled on the bed frames but to no avail - they were solidly fixed into the wall. Mike looked at Peter who returned the glance and then winced.

Not a word was spoken between them. The other Venturers just sat quietly on the cell floor. Most had their knees pulled up and were resting their heads on their bare knees. Mike thought about Scott and how he was holding up. Of all the boys to separate, Scott was not a good choice. He was gentle, had a small frame and loved company. He was not a loner, nor overly adventurous. Scott was good intellectually, but was not the strongest boy in the unit. He was a doer but had never really been pushed to the limit.

Mike started to think of how he would handle the Russians if they returned. He walked up to the black metal door and examined it again. A peephole was cut about level with the average man's chin. Mike pushed his fingers into the circle of the hole and slid the cover to one side. He strained to see up the corridor in both directions.

Mike called for quiet and cocked his ear to the hole. Nothing. No men's voices. No moving around elsewhere. No motors whirring. Nothing. This was not looking or sounding good. In his mind Mike was war-gaming scenarios. He often mind-mapped problems and tried to sort them out without putting pen to paper. He was becoming quite adept at the practice. His real fear was the nothingness. If he could hear nothing, then maybe no one outside the jail could hear them either.

'Therefore,' he thought, 'he needed something visual to attract attention.' He looked at each of the boys. They were dressed for a swim. They had no matches or lighters. There was nothing in the cell to start a fire. Maybe Scott had something in his cell. He walked to the window wall.

130

"Scott!" Mike yelled at the top of his voice.

"Hell Mike! You scared the daylights out of us," Peter said.

"Sorry fellows. I should have told you first," Mike said. "I'm going to try again ... Scott!"

Scott heard his name being called but couldn't discern who was calling. He went to the door and opened it slowly, while on his knees, and he slid out to the balcony. He heard Mike call the second time. Gingerly, Scott knelt up and surveyed the scene below. He couldn't see anyone anywhere and he decided to take a chance.

"Mike, is that you?" Scott yelled back.

"Yes! Are you okay?"

"Yes!"

"Do you have anything in your cell to start a fire?"

Scott knew he had to be careful. What if the Russians were still around when he told Mike where he was? All plans for escape would be dashed. He decided to lie.

"No! There is nothing here," Scott yelled.

"Okay!" Mike replied.

The other Venturers seemed happy to hear from Scott and the conversation in the cell picked up. It went quiet again when Mike sat down.

Scott knew if he waited until dark for the main lantern to switch on, it could be too late. He decided to take a gamble. Slowly he worked his way back into the control room. He had made a cutting of a fleur de lis or the three-fingered Scout salute. In the lighthouse keeper's drawers he had not only found paper, pens and scissors but also some sticky tape. He placed his cut-out on the outside of the revolving glass pane and stuck it down with tape. Next he climbed down to where the control switches were and turned off the automatic override switch. This allowed him to operate the main lantern manually. He then turned on the main motor and the room began to fill with noise as the lantern slowly burst into life, like a movie projector, and its revolving parts began to move.

Scott went back to the desk and put all his bits and pieces back where they belonged. He checked the trapdoor to ensure it was still locked and then looked for a hiding place. He knew once the Russians saw the light on they would come looking for him, or more particularly, look for a way to shut off the light and so stop drawing attention to the place.

What Scott didn't know is that the lighthouse had been wired with special sensors. The moment he threw on the switch, an alarm rang in the Maritime Services department's building in Sydney. An operator in a special room with a statewide map dotted with coloured lights representing the various lighthouses was walking between desks when he noticed the flashing light.

"Gaye, we may have a malfunction at number seven," Frank Smith said to his partner, Gaye Donahue.

"Tap the light and then the board to see if the globe is going," Gaye replied.

Frank started walking towards the board when he remembered something.

"Tap nothing. These globes are those new million-hour globes and they were only changed a couple of weeks ago."

Gaye looked at her younger colleague and nodded.

"You're right. I'd say give it a couple of minutes in case the system rights itself or old Luke the lighthouse keeper realises his light is on and switches it off. In which case we should expect a call from him to tell us what happened, in a few minutes," Gaye said.

Gaye looked at Frank and then studied the board. Most of the state's lighthouses had been converted to automatic power some years ago. A few retained lighthouse keepers who had switched jobs to become live-in historians until their contracts ran out. This helped maintain the lighthouses and also keep the vandals away.

Myall Lakes lighthouse was no different except ... it had a lighthouse keeper who was being retained almost as a full-time keeper from yesteryear. He was informative of the weather patterns and also the tides and various sea states. The local council was trying to find some way to retain his services long after his time was up as a lighthouse keeper and the lighthouse operated fully on automatic.

"Frank, if Luke doesn't call in another minute ring him and see what is going on," Gaye said.

"Okay, mate."

The Russians were having a hard time getting their boat to work. Vitali had tried everything he could - barring pulling the engine apart.

"Comrades, this will not work. I think we had better find another way out of here," Vitali said.

Boris and Dimitri stopped in their tracks. They had wanted to give up some time ago but kept going because of Vitali, their leader, their boss.

"Da," Boris said. "We should just cover the boat, get our love packages and get out of here."

"What about those boys?" Dimitri asked.

"What about them? We leave them where they are and we keep moving," Vitali said.

"They have no water, no food and no way of escaping," Dimitri said. "If we get caught and the authorities find out we left the boys to die we will surely hang for it."

Vitali looked at both of his offsiders in turn. "Okay, when we get back to a city we call the police and tell them where to find the boys, they can last for a while," Vitali said.

The three agreed and started covering up the craft. Within a few minutes it was if the boat had vanished. The Russians started walking back to the lighthouse.

CHAPTER THIRTY-ONE

Scott became quite concerned his actions would really cause his demise. He went to the balcony once more and gingerly peered over the railings in a number of locations. He could see no one in the area. This meant either the Russians had left, or were inside the jail ... somewhere. He decided he had to take a chance. If he stayed in the dome area he was totally cornered and it would not take the Russians long to find him.

Scott retraced his way into the machine room and across to the trapdoor. It was locked from underneath. He wriggled the lift-up, recessed handle to ensure the door was fastened securely. The youth ran his eyes slowly along the seams of the door and had an idea. He went to the drawers in the lighthouse keeper's desk and found a small bread knife the lighthouse keeper must use to make his lunch or cut his fruit when he was in the dome for long periods. The deft teenager cocked his ear to the trapdoor to ensure there was no movement the other side. He worked the knife along the edge where the lock was located and started trying to slide the blade over the lock's tongue.

A few moments later and the lock gave way. Scott quietly and slowly lifted the trapdoor. On the other side was a steep ladder bolted to the wall. He leant down and looked through the trapdoor. No sound and no one was there.

It was now or never. Scott was worried he would get caught by the Russians before he had time to find an escape route or check on Mike and the other Venturers. He lifted open the trapdoor and climbed down the ladder. On the way through he pushed the tongue of the lock back into its casing and it stayed there. Next, he pulled the door back into place. This way, if he needed to retreat he had somewhere to go. Scott quietly continued down the ladder and onto firm flooring. He was on the top landing of a large, spiral stairway that led down to a corridor and his former cell. Every footstep Scott made seemed to echo in his mind.

There was no audible sound, just his mind playing tricks because of the danger. He made it to the landing where he had been taken earlier by the Russians. 'This was bizarre,' he thought. 'Fancy a colonial government building a lighthouse out of a jail!'

The passageway ahead was empty and no noise issued from it. He quickly hurried along the corridor. Then something made him stop. He looked at the cell he had just passed and recognised it as his! Yes, there was the paint scraping on the outside wall that acted as a marker.

He pushed the peephole cover to the side and peered inside. The sight sent shivers up his spine. This was meant to be his holding pen. His cell. His prison. 'To hell with this,' he thought, 'let's get out of here!' He replaced the swinging peephole and kept padding his way along the corridor to the next set of stairs. A rush of cool air hit him as he stopped and listened for any intruders.

The muffled voices of a group of people were below him somewhere. Scott tensed as he knew he was now heading towards danger. His heart started thumping faster and his breath became shallower as he tried to melt into the walls. He worked his way down to the next level and peered around the corner. No one was there! The noises became louder and he decided to wait and listen and check out his options. There weren't many – run back up the stairs and climb the ladder and close the trapdoor; give himself up or slip into any cell that may be unlocked and try and hide behind a door.

He made his way along the corridor and found Mike's cell. It was padlocked from the outside like his. Drats! The Russians had used one of the old, large Jackson-style brass padlocks to keep the outside door bolt in place. He may have tampered with a lock in the dome, but this was different. The Jacksons were used by prison authorities in New South Wales for decades with great success. He gently knocked on the door.

"Mike, it's Scott," he said in a voice barely above a whisper.

His words went through the cell like an electric current.

Immediate quiet fell on the cell. Mike rushed to the peephole. Before he could open it, the metal cover slid away and the face of a teenage angel stared at him.

'How the hell ... ? Are you okay? Where are the Russians?" Mike babbled out. This was the first time Scott had ever caught Mike lost for coherent words.

The rest of the boys crowded around Mike and craned to hear every word.

"Shhh! It's Scott!" someone yelled before being told to keep quiet.

"Mike, I was able to squeeze through the bars and climb to the engine room above," Scott whispered.

"Is he okay? Where are the Russians," Peter asked.

"Scott, keep going. Can you get us out of here?" Mike asked.

"I don't know where the Russians are. I am just going to try and find out if I can get some help. Your door, and the one next door with the other Venturers, is padlocked from the outside and will take a huge sledge hammer to break them – never mind the noise,"

Scott said. "Mike, I have set in motion two ways to attract attention."

Mike craned his ear to the hole.

"I have turned on the lighthouse beam and erected a flag upside down, someone is bound to come around now," Scott said.

Mike was astounded. This was not the shy boy he had first taken under his wing. This was a young man showing his prowess as a Venturer, and someone with a lot of mettle. Mike signalled to the other Venturers to keep quiet.

"Scott, you'll have to find out where the Russians are and see if you can get to a phone and call the police," Mike said. "It may be some time before passers-by see the flag and beam. By the way, well done Scott! You're a champion," the Venturer leader said.

The other Venturers started whispering a chorus, "Well done Scott! Well done Scott!" Scott's eyes had started to moisten as his leader and mentor spoke to him. When he heard his Venturers singing to him, that was the end of it emotionally. Tears began to well up inside him and then run gently down his cheeks. Scott had to get away from here. He steeled himself and told Mike he would keep moving and find out what he could before returning. Scott replaced the peephole and continued down the corridor. A loud cheer rang out as Mike finished relaying to the Venturers what Scott had done.

"That explains why he wouldn't yell out," Mark said. "He didn't want to draw attention to himself until he set in motion a signalling system. Clever kid!"

Mike and the others looked at Mark and laughed. He then signalled them to be quiet as he went through some contingency plans in case the Russians came into the cell.

Boris cleared the bush area first. He saw the lighthouse and started walking towards it when he stopped.

"Quick, come here! We have problems," he said hurriedly.

Vitali and Dimitri caught up and looked at the lighthouse. This was not good. The light was on and so – there was someone home!

A flag had been erected too. The Russians looked at each other. Vitali gripped his handgun.

"Show no mercy! The boys have escaped. We have to take them out before we get our love packages," Vitali said angrily.

"Any mass-killing of the boys will throw a national hunt for us into action," Dimitri observed.

"What do you think we should do? Run now and abandon our love packages?" Vitali asked through clenched teeth.

"No. I also can't see how the boys would have escaped. Their cells were bolted and locked," Vitali said. "Therefore, there must be someone else in the lighthouse, someone we never saw."

Dimitri looked at his boss.

"Comrade, if we move quickly we can recover our packages and escape. There is plenty of bushland to shield us before we hit the highway," he said.

"No. We need to tidy up by leaving no witnesses. You haven't gone soft comrade? Have you?" Boris asked.

Both Dimitri and Vitali looked at Boris and winced. They knew they were now in an impossible position and they had to kill innocent, unarmed teenage boys to keep alive themselves.

CHAPTER THIRTY-TWO

Scott made his way through the jail listening at each open space and working his way forward. The door to the main office was closed and locked with a sliding bolt and padlock. Scott crept near it but heard no movement or voices inside. He went to the main entrance and saw the front gate – something was not right. His eyes scoured the courtyard and then the gate again. A chain had been placed through two open handhold areas. However, an open lock held the chains in place.

Scott thought about it for a moment. When the Russians brought the Venturers here they did not replace the chain through any gate. Maybe the Russians had left? He walked to the gate and peered through the open handhold area. His view took him to the edge of the water and hinterland. He was about to go back inside when he caught a glimpse of three men walking towards the jail. Scott's heart skipped a beat as he realised it was the Russians returning!

Instinctively, Scott closed the lock on the chain and ran into the main entranceway. He started closing the door then he became riveted to the floor. A phone in the locked main office was ringing. Brrring! Brrring! Brrring!

It finally stopped. 'No one else must be here,' he thought. The office had a solid door and was locked. He couldn't get in to use the phone and ring the police. Scott closed the door to the main entrance and went walking along the corridor looking for something to prop up against the door.

"Gaye, there's no answer at Myall Lake so I have rung the local police. They're sending someone to check it out," Frank said to his boss.

"Thanks mate. You may want to alert local shipping the light seems to be malfunctioning," Gaye said.

"Okay boss," Frank said as he went back to his desk.

Constable Rugless had a feeling he would be drawn deeply into the saga of the missing boys and the hush-hush operation involving the Federal police and Customs. When his sergeant directed him to guard the bus, he was told the federal agents were part of a secret operation involving Customs. The plot was beginning to unfold.

Constable Rugless had walked around the bus a number of times and had seen the trail of footprints and the drag marks of surfboards leading to the sea. He had been instructed to touch nothing associated with the bus until the investigators and Federal agents had arrived. It was not fair. 'These kids, whoever they are, could be in a world of hurt,' and he could do nothing to assist. 'Then again,' he thought, 'the kids could have been operating with a boat owner and gone for a day's outing.' The only issue would be to give the bus driver a warning about parking on the beach. His police senses got the better of him and he went to the back of the trailer behind the bus.

Constable Rugless pulled down the zippered side and peered in. Hanging in the rear of the trailer, were a number of blue coloured Scout uniforms with maroon yokes across the shoulders and blue scarves with double-white piping. He had seen this uniform before but he couldn't work out where. 'Had he arrested a teenage Scout? What do they call them? Venturers! That's it!' No, no Venturers had come under his notice. He had seen the uniform before, 'Somewhere in a picture maybe?'

He was standing looking at the uniform and didn't notice, or hear, the car pull up. Two men dressed in very neat civilian slacks, short sleeves and shoes approached.

"Good morning constable," one said.

Constable Rugless wheeled round and saw the two men looking at him. One slowly produced an Australian Federal Police badge and the introductions began.

"Hi, I'm Federal Agent Barry Walters and this is my partner Federal Agent Heath Lomax," the taller agent said.

Constable Rugless introduced himself and said he was checking to see what was inside the trailer in case it helped identify who had left it.

"Thanks constable. We'll take it from here," Lomax said. "Oh, by the way ... you need to contact your station."

"Thanks. I'll leave you to it," Constable Rugless said and then returned to his car.

The radio reception was still bad, so Constable Rugless drove to higher ground. He had made his way to a headland north of the lighthouse and radioed in.

"Shayne, there seems to be some problem at the lighthouse," Sergeant Sullivan reported. "You had better go and check it out."

"Any idea of what sort of problems Sarge?" Constable Rugless asked.

"We had a call from Maritime Services telling us the main light used for shipping had been activated. It may just be a fault, in which case we'll call your good friend the lighthouse keeper to look at it," Sergeant Sullivan replied.

"Or it could be a group of missing Venturers up to no good. I'll check it out," Constable Rugless said as he started driving back to the lighthouse.

It wasn't that far back to the lighthouse. However, the journey wound its way through hinterland and dense scrubland. Constable Rugless decided to check out a nearby headland and view the lighthouse from afar. He got out of the car and walked to the rear of the police car. Out of the boot he retrieved a pair of high-powered binoculars.

He approached the headland clearing slowly and raised his binoculars towards the southern coastline. The white lighthouse stood out like a sore thumb. It sat perched on some of the area's best seaside land. The view out to sea and up and down the coast from the lighthouse was unsurpassable. It would have made a great place for a jail as a lot of the work had been carried out by convicts in the local area.

This work included a large sea ramp comprising thousands of large rocks and a few small rock bridges over some streams. Atop the flagpole Constable Rugless noticed the Australian flag was flying upside down. Constable Rugless got back in his car and radioed in. Now he was sure something more was afoot than just a group of missing Venturers. His sergeant told him to stay put until backup could be organised. He was to radio in progress reports if he observed anything in the meantime.

Scott picked up his pace and checked every open door he could. He was worried about the Russians and what they would do when they found the gates and door locked. In an open cell Scott found some minor maintenance tools and two stools. 'These must have been for the workmen,' he thought to himself. A smile came over his face as he rummaged through the tools for anything useful.

The irony of trying to lock someone out of the jail instead of in had dawned on the teenager. He chuckled to himself. Scott picked up some tools and ran back to the main entrance doors. They were bolted from the inside, in a similar manner to the cells. Adrenalin was flowing through Scott as he slid the bolt and then forced a screwdriver through the hole that had been left for a padlock. He turned to run when he heard a shot ring out. Suddenly, Scott took flight as he ran at breakneck speed through the corridors to Mike's cell. He pushed open the peephole to be greeted with Mike's left eye staring at him.

"Are you okay?" Mike said excitedly. "We heard a shot."

"Yes. I'm fine," Scott finally managed to bleat out, as he was still breathless from the run. "I found a spanner and screwdriver. Maybe these can help."

Scott tried attacking the lock with both tools but to no avail. A cacophony of voices could be heard near the front door.

"Don't worry, I bolted the door," Scott said. "They'll have to almost bulldoze their way through."

Mike watched Scott work and tried to keep his voice calm.

"We came in through the front door, the Russians will probably want to do it again. We are their live witnesses and somewhere in here are their drugs. They won't leave until they have their packages," Mike said.

Scott looked at Mike. 'Maybe that was the key,' he thought.

"How about I find those packages in case we have to use them as a bargaining chip?" Scott asked.

Peter was trying to keep the noise from the Venturers down so Mike and Scott could talk. He saw the worried look on Mike's face. He watched while his leader gripped his own hands out of sight of Scott, forcing himself to be calm. Peter knew Mike was trying not to scare Scott. Mike was hoping not to baulk him as Scott worked to free them.

"Scott, if you found the drugs and a way of giving them to the Russians without letting them back in, they will probably leave," Mike said.

Scott stopped working on the lock and looked up at Mike.

"I think I know how to do it. Mike, I'll have to go in case they find a way to break in. Back soon," he said as he looked at Mike.

That was a look that would stay with Mike for the rest of his life. Scott was trying to control his emotions and also show he was resourceful. The blonde teenager was scared and was running on adrenalin. Mike wished he could be in Scott's shoes instead of the teenager. He wanted to give Scott his years of experience - but he could only send his thoughts through the ether. Scott by now had run off.

Constable Rugless heard the shot and saw three men near the front gate of the jail. He radioed in an urgent report and said he would get closer to the jail for a better view.

The look on Boris's face said it all. When the three Russians were confronted with a locked jail gate, he became enraged. He pulled out his pistol and fired at the padlock – movie-style. The problem was, this was not a movie. The 9mm round had lodged in the padlock and had not blasted it open as is the case in police movies. Dimitri would have laughed, however, seeing his boss so enraged he felt compelled to bite his tongue instead.

"Stand back and I'll take out a link instead," Boris said.

Dimitri and Vitali stood back and grimaced while they waited for the second shot to ring out. BANG! Boris was on target this time. The third link from the lock was blown away. The smell of cordite from the shooting hung in the air. Vitali pulled the chain through the gate and pushed on the heavy timber. The gate opened and the three men gingerly entered.

Boris indicated to Dimitri to go to the left and for Vitali to go to the right. Between them and the entrance to the jail and lighthouse was a dirt and rock courtyard. The men fanned out and started approaching the building stealthily. All three were partly crouched, scouring their surrounds as they moved forward to the main building – looking for whoever had tried to lock them out.

Scott had heard the second shot. The sound of metal smashing metal echoed everywhere. His heartbeat climbed an extra few ratchets to push even more adrenalin through the boy's body.

'If I brought a collection of packages in here, where would I hide them?' Scott thought to himself. The Russians had brought their drugs into the jail when they marched the boys from the boat. They had put them down while they found cells for Mike, the other Venturers and Scott. Scott's mind had not been on locating packages when he escaped from the lighthouse area. Now his focus was intense. He ran away from Mike's cell back towards the stairs leading to the lighthouse.

It was familiar territory. Though this was not the answer. The cells along the way had virtually all been locked except where he found the tools and there were no packages in there. Scott saw the beginning of the stairs leading to the lighthouse and knew he had gone too far. Better to double back and re-check the cells. While he started doing this, his mind went into overdrive. Bingo! If all the cells were closed then maybe the second of the two offices near the main entrance was open! One office was locked. This was where he heard the phone ring. The second could have been already locked, but he couldn't remember.

When Mike heard the second shot he went quiet. Mark put his hand on his shoulder and told him not to worry too much as Scott was resourceful. Mike gripped Mark's hand and thanked him. He gathered the Venturers around him and asked them to silently pray for Scott and themselves.

The three Russians regrouped at the front door. Their obstacle was different this time – there was no chain or bolt on the outside. A large keyhole was present but none of them had the huge key to fit into it.

"Give me a hand to knock the door open," Boris ordered.

The three men stepped back and then simultaneously pushed their shoulders to the door. All three bounced back without the door budging an inch. They tried it again twice before stopping to think things through.

"It has to be bolted from the inside," Dimitri said as he rubbed his shoulder. "I don't think you can shoot your way in this time."

Boris looked flushed. He was the one empowered. His group had the weapons – not the boys. That is, if it was the boys who had escaped.

"It can't be the boys or the adult," Vitali said. "We put them in cells, bolted the doors and put padlocks on them. They would have to be modern day Houdinis to have escaped."

"I don't believe it is the boys. I think someone else has got inside, found the boys and locked us out," Boris said. "Our real questions are; how do we break into a convict jail? And who else is inside?"

Dimitri stepped back from the doorway and suggested they could probably bluff their way into retrieving the drugs. He said if they shouted at the main door that no one will be touched if the packages are handed over it may stir whoever was inside into action. Boris agreed and stated he would start the yelling while the other two looked for another way in. Perhaps through a window, or over a wall into the rear courtyard? His team mates looked at him and nodded. They then started making their way along either side of the building.

"No one will be hurt if you open the door and give us our packages!" Boris yelled at the front door.

"Tell me who you are and what you want! We just want to go away from here with our packages. Come on out - you'll be safe!" he added loudly.

Nothing stirred. No sound could be heard. Boris tried again with a similar message but to no avail. Dimitri and Vitali found the going tough. How do you scale six-metre-high walls with no ladder or other equipment? It was not easy to break in – even harder to break out.

Scott had hurriedly made his way back to the main entrance doorway. He stood frozen as he heard Boris taunt him with his 'safe' message.

'Do I reply and give part of the game away? Or do I stay silent and keep working?' Scott asked himself.

He checked the front door. The bolt was in place and the doors secure. The office on the left where Scott heard the phone ring was locked. The one on the right had a bolt in place but no lock. Scott slid back the bolt slowly, trying not to make any noise. He pushed the door open slowly and saw the ten packages piled on a table. The Venturer's boogie boards were also neatly stacked against a wall. This was an interesting room. It had a fireplace and tall mantelpiece set in the centre wall. There were no windows for natural light. At either end of the table was a chair.

Around the walls were glass cabinets filled with record books of the inmates who had served time, their recorded punishments and an officers' roster. Scott marveled at the penmanship and beautiful copperplate writing. It was so different to the scrawls he was used to seeing everyday on his and other students' books. There was no phone in the room. No wall socket for a phone either. Communication with the outside world would be nigh impossible.

Scott investigated the packages more closely. Each was rectangular in shape and was wrapped in waterproof material. All were sealed. The question now was what to do with them. There was no way Scott would open any door or window for the Russians and just hand them the packages. That action could be tantamount to his own death or that of

Mike's and the Venturers. The problem was how to get the packages to the Russians and still be safe until help arrived - if help arrived.

Both Dimitri and Boris checked the length of the courtyard walls looking for some way in to the jail. There was none. The walls were nearly a metre thick and six metres high. There were no ladders to be seen or trees to climb up to assist. The Russians seemed caught in a time warp, made by convicts two centuries before, with only controlled ways in and out of the prison. They started making their way back to Vitali.

CHAPTER THIRTY-THREE

Police patrol cars with sirens blaring drove at breakneck speed to meet up with Constable Rugless on his headland vantage point. He had heard the second shot and called for well-armed backup. The two Federal agents Constable Rugless had met on the beach were among the police team that arrived.

Constable Rugless briefed the various plain-clothes detectives and uniformed police as they arrived. Detectives had been called in as they were members of specialist, elite squads that only functioned during major problems. A discussion between the Federal agents and Constable Rugless ensued. It was plainly stated that as the jail was State property, it was up to the State police to resolve the situation. If the situation developed into a terrorist activity, then the Federal police would take over and the Special Air Service Regiment called in – if required. The lines of engagement had been drawn.

Constable Rugless took out sheets of paper from his boot and started drawing diagrams of the prison as he knew it. Police were separately trying to contact the lighthouse keeper to bring him to the forward command post where Constable Rugless was located.

The police teams saw the lighthouse beam on and the Australian flag flying upside down. The consensus among the police was that vandals had more than likely broken into the jail and switched on the light. The second possibility was; the flag had been placed upside down by people who didn't know better. Constable Rugless never accepted these arguments. He strongly believed the Venturers had somehow got caught up with the Russians.

Scott scoured the opened office. There was no way to communicate with the Russians except by yelling through the door and Scott didn't want to try it. He figured he would be giving away too much information and he could be tricked into saying or doing something he didn't want to. Scott picked up the packages and decided to take them aloft. He figured he had a better chance of controlling the situation from the lighthouse operations area. He walked quickly past Mike and the Venturers' cell and along the corridors. There was no time to tell Mike everything. Anyway, Scott wanted to ensure Mike wasn't aware of his movements in the event the Russians were to quiz him on Scott's whereabouts.

The weight of the 'love' packages were much too heavy for Scott to climb back up the ladder to the control room in one go. He left the packages at the bottom of the ladder, climbed up and started working on the lock with the knife he had found inside earlier. The lock's tongue slid back into its recess and the youth was able to raise the trapdoor. Scott secured the door in the upright position and then climbed down.

He repeated the climb a number of times to take all the packages upstairs. Scott closed the trapdoor. He looked around for something to put over the door to jam it shut in case the Russians made it into the jail and went looking for him. The only moveable objects were the table and chairs used by the lighthouse keeper. Scott pushed these on top of the trapdoor.

'Now what to do?' Scott thought to himself. He had turned on the lighthouse beam earlier and this was still working. He had also hoisted the flag upside down. So far, no one had taken any notice. Scott sat down on the floor with his back to the wall and tried to mind map what had happened. He then had to try and work out another way of attracting attention.

Boris and the other two Russians were having a hard time. They could not find a way into the jail. The walls were too high to climb without grappling hooks and ropes or ladders; also, the front doors were closed and locked from the inside. The lighthouse itself was quite formidable, as there seemed no way to scale the outside wall and climb to the top.

"We have to get in through the front doors," Dimitri said. "All other ways into the jail are beyond us. We would need a circus troupe here to help us or the Spetsnaz."

Boris looked at his two compatriots in turn.

"There must be a way to get in that even the Spetsnaz or other Russian special forces could conquer," he said.

"What about the tools on the boat? Can we use them? What about the fuel on the boat? Can we use it to blow a hole in the door?" Boris asked anxiously.

Dimitri thought for a moment and suggested that the tools on the boat could probably assist in leveraging the hinges from the door. Vitali took a different tack and stated that the fuel could be used to blow a hole through the two doors. However, he added, they would have to work out the best way to prime or ignite it so as to cause maximum damage to the doors.

"Go back to the boat. Get the gear you need and hurry back. I'll keep trying to talk to whoever is inside and find out who they are. Maybe we can have them behind the door when you are ready to blow it!" Boris said with a smile.

Dimitri and Vitali agreed and started heading back to their concealed boat. Boris leaned into the doors and kept trying to engage whoever had locked the trio out.

"Don't you realise you have nowhere to go?" Boris told the doors. "Just give us our packages and we'll leave – that's all we want."

Scott decided to have another look around the control area. Earlier, he had found the switches for the main beam and turned them on. However, he thought to himself, there were a lot of switches and maybe he could do something else to attract attention. Scott opened the main control boxes and recovered a booklet on the operating system from the table drawer. A solution soon dawned on Scott. The trouble was, it was risky as it may panic the Russians.

He made his way up to the verandah level, slowly opened the door and went outside. Scott peered over the railing for a glance to see what the Russians were doing and where they were located. He had to crawl to a few different locations before he saw the main jail gates. In the distance two men could be seen walking towards the hinterland.

'That leaves one,' Scott thought to himself. 'Now, something to keep them away. What is it Mike says? Divide and conquer.'

Scott crawled back to the lantern room door. He looked up and saw the flag hanging limply as there was no wind. He looked back over the balcony and saw a pair of megaphone-type speakers mounted on an extended arm on the top of a structure around fifty metres south of the lighthouse. Scott's imagination fired up. He crawled back into the lantern room and grabbed the operating manual again. Could the speakers help him? Or, if he could get them working, would they cause more problems for himself and the other Venturers?

Scott rifled through the manual and found some photos of the speakers. They were foghorn sirens that blasted out a shrill noise as a warning to shipping during periods of heavy fog. Each fog siren had its own noise sequence. This one was set to go off every ninety seconds with three blasts. Scott took the book to the operating level where all the switches and motors were located.

'Damn!' thought Scott as he read the manual. 'This lighthouse has an antiquated motor system to manually drive the sirens.' He flicked a few more pages and then realised the lighthouse had been upgraded to electrical switches to run the sirens. He opened a number of switch cover doors and ran his eyes over the labels and checked them against the photos in the manual. Staring him in the face were two large control knobs; a red one and a green one. Above them was a small sign that read Fog Horn Siren.

Scott held his breath and pushed the green knob. Almost immediately, an extremely loud siren blared out with three blasts. According to the manual, the noise would be heard for a few kilometres out to sea. Never mind the immediate vicinity. The siren had an instant response from several different camps.

Dimitri and Vitali initially froze and looked at each other as they were walking towards the boat. They backtracked to the beginning of the clearing to observe the jail. No change. They decided to run to the boat and then to the lighthouse. The noise would have to attract local resident and police action. Therefore, a noose was starting to be fitted around their necks. The question was did they have time to blow the jail doors, retrieve their packages and escape before they were cornered or should they cut their losses and run now?

"We can't run now," Dimitri said. "If anything happens to Boris we could all swing for it."

Vitali looked at Dimitri.

"You are right. But if the cops get to the jail before we do we may have to rethink things. Do you agree?" Vitali asked.

Dimitri was perspiring for the first time and nodded.

"Da, Boris will still be a key and we need to keep factoring him in," Dimitri said.

The men picked up their pace as they ran through the brush towards their covered boat.

"What the hell was that?" Federal Agent Heath Lomax asked as he craned his neck towards the lighthouse.

"It's the fog siren. It alerts shipping off the coastline when heavy fog rolls in," Constable Rugless said. "I haven't heard it go off for quite some time."

Federal Agent Walters kept his binoculars to his face and chimed in, "Well something seems to have changed at the jail. I can't see any movement but it sounds like someone upped the ante down there."

Constable Rugless only heard half the conversation as he was getting back into his car so he could radio his bosses with the update. While he was on the radio the fog horn siren sounded again.

"What was that?" his sergeant asked.

"Boss, that's the foghorn siren. It normally only sounds when a heavy fog is in the area," Constable Rugless said.

"Sounds like someone is really trying to draw attention to the lighthouse. Now is probably the time to send a few cars to the jail. You'll need to have some with sirens first and others silently following," the Inspector said.

The two police discussed their tactics before Constable Rugless held a meeting with all the police present at his command post. When the foghorn siren sounded, Boris was jolted where he stood. He now knew for sure someone was in the control room of the lighthouse. He walked back towards the main gates to get a better view of the lighthouse.

"Good game little one, or whoever you are. But you can't win!" Boris shouted. "Throw the packages down to me and we'll leave now!"

Scott was sitting on the floor of the operations room when he heard Boris yell out. He could probably end this now if he threw the packages over the side of the verandah. However, there were no guarantees he wouldn't be shot anyway as he tried to throw the Russians' stash. How could he survive then if he was wounded? Not a pleasant thought. Scott went through the jail in his mind. He went over his actions in detail. Were Mike and the Venturers safe? Could the Russians get in to the jail? If they could, how long before Mike and the Venturers would be shot or hurt by the Russians? How long would it take the Russians to get to him? Scott's mind began processing the information like a computer as he tried to solve each question and think ahead.

If he threw the packages over the railing and they broke open on impact, would this rile the Russians sufficiently for them to start shooting at him? Phew! The youth was starting to get hot and edgy. He mind mapped his options before returning to the lighthouse keeper's desk. The Russians were more than hot and edgy – they were infuriated! These were three men who had served in conflicts overseas with the Russian forces – how they could they be in this predicament?

CHAPTER THIRTY-FOUR

Rear Admiral Drew Curry rang his friend Admiral Chris Ramage once more.

"Chris, it won't be long now. We have the Eastralia and Lady Yvonne only hours away from being within radar sighting of the Pushkin," Curry said. "The Black Hawks offloaded their special cargo on Eastralia and all is ready for the final showdown."

"Drew thanks, this will be a day we will all savor as we finally bring some good news to the prime minister. That is, if all goes well."

"Fingers crossed Chris. The next bird overhead in the area is due within the hour. I'll keep you in touch."

The two admirals rang off. Chris Ramage knew he was on a good wicket with HMAS Eastralia. It was an impressive frigate armed with a five and a quarter inch (127 mm) gun; eight missiles, six torpedoes and a complement of 170 personnel. It also had a Seasprite helicopter aboard which could be used to deliver the members of the SASR aboard the Pushkin as required.

Admiral Ramage called Commander O'Shea into his office.

"Chris, call Inspector Dave Farrell and let him know we should have visibility of the Pushkin within the next hour or so."

"Aye, sir," Commander O'Shea said as he returned to his office to make the call.

Constable Rugless had ordered a patrol car with sirens blaring to go to the lighthouse. The cars were accompanied by the two Federal agents. Constable Rugless then ordered a second car to patrol the highway and side road entrances leading back to the lighthouse. Sergeant Sullivan had already called for the Water Police to assist with a water presence.

Vitali was running out of patience. His plan to pick up the ten love packages had been thwarted so far, and he was in the invidious position of having to try and break into a jail to rescue his white powder of death.

The police siren could just be heard on the top of the small breeze that was blowing in from the south. Boris ran towards the gate and kept looking at the lighthouse. He was searching for some human movement. The foghorn siren was now starting to really irritate him and he was ready to shoot the loud speaker from its post when his two counterparts ran through main gate. Dimitri was carrying the metal fuel tank of the boat and Boris, a tool box.

"How many have escaped? Where are they comrade? We have little time as the police are on their way," Dimitri said anxiously.

Vitali looked at him with pure disdain. Dimitri had not caused this problem but Vitali wanted someone to blame. His face contorted but he bit his tongue before answering his comrade.

"I have been calling out but no one has answered. I will give them one last try before we blow the doors and retrieve our packages," Vitali said.

Boris rifled through the toolbox looking for anything that may assist in opening the massive, wooden doors. There was nothing big or strong enough to prise the doors open. Only a fire or explosion would do it.

"Stand back Vitali. I'll use the fuel tank as a bomb and shoot it. The explosion should rip the doors off the hinges," Dimitri said.

He placed the metal fuel tank near the doors and turned to walk back when a shout echoed out from above.

"Hey down there!" Scott shouted. "Do you want your love packages?"

Boris walked out of the building's shadow and into the open. Dimitri and Vitali took a wider berth and also walked out to the open to look up at the verandah around the lighthouse.

"Who are you?" Boris asked.

Scott stayed under the verandah railing and continued to yell out. He was initially worried the Russians would shoot him if he showed himself. The gangly youth peered through the cracks in the railing and pinpointed Boris. He could just see the sides of the other two, but they were not in full view.

"It doesn't matter who I am. I have your packages and am prepared to give them to you ... but only if you leave," Scott said.

"Open the doors and give them to us and we'll leave," Vitali said as he walked backwards towards the main gate to try and get a better view of the verandah.

The foghorn siren kept sounding and the police sirens could now be heard wailing continuously at low volume to indicate they were still some way off.

"I can't open the doors but I'll throw your packages down to you," Scott said.

"No. If you do that they will break and be useless to us. Just open the doors, let us get the packages and we'll leave you in peace," Vitali said.

"No. If you want the packages the three of you will need to catch them. They are not that heavy and you are all pretty big men," Scott said as he manoeuvred the packages closer to him.

Dimitri motioned to Boris.

"That's the kid we put in the lighthouse. How the hell did he escape? I closed and locked his cell. There was no way out through the door," Dimitri said.

"Maybe he broke out of the bars and just flew up to the boardwalk," Vitali returned scathingly. "Are you sure it's him?"

"I'm pretty sure. We just need to verify it. Call him to stand up and we'll soon find out," Dimitri said.

"Hey Blondie! Stand up so we can see you," Vitali called.

"No. The police are on their way and will be here soon. Your only way out of here is to catch the packages and make a run for it," Scott said. "If I were you, I'd tell your men to stand in the open if they don't want to lose these packages. I'm throwing the first one now."

Scott picked up the first package and lobbed it over the railing at Boris. The Russian flinched and caught it awkwardly with his pistol still in his hand. Dimitri and Vitali moved out to the open as they realised Scott meant what he said. They put their handguns in their rolled-down wetsuits. Scott flung two more packages which made Vitali and Dimitri scurry to catch them.

He threw two more in quick succession and had the Russians virtually dancing to catch them. Scott was suddenly in charge. He knew this would soon turn to anger on the part of the Russians, but he had to complete what he started to help bring an end to the situation that he and the Venturers had never asked to be placed in.

The police sirens began to get louder and the Russians were becoming very anxious. Scott tossed two more packages and waited.

"Hurry! We need to go!" Boris yelled at Scott.

Vitali placed the packages in three piles ready for the men to pick up and run with when the last one was thrown. Scott looked through the railing cracks to check where the Russians were standing. He noticed Dimitri motion to Boris and point towards the jail. Boris shook his head. Scott knew something was not right. This was like playing the last hand in poker with both players believing they hold the winning hand.

"Once I throw these last packages, will you go?" Scott yelled.

"Yes, yes. Now hurry. Our time is short," Vitali said anxiously.

He spoke quietly in Russian to Dimitri and told him to blast the doors before they left so the police would face a diversion before trying to chase them. Dimitri nodded.

Scott took a deep breath. He reached carefully for the packages and in quick succession lobbed the last ones over the railing with a spin. The Russians each outstretched their hands and reached for their final love packages. It was like a scene from a movie playing in slow motion.

The Russians caught the packages and fumbled with them as Scott's spin had forced them to tumble more than the last seven. Scott peered intently through the railing cracks and forced his breathing as he watched the Russians fumble and then grip the packages. He steeled himself.

"What have you done? What is this on this package? Aaah! I cannot free my hands!" Vitali screamed out as he violently shook the package in a vain attempt to dislodge his hands from the superglued wrapping.

Boris and Dimitri were in the same position and were swearing in Russian. All three men were dancing around as they tried to remove their hands from the package wrapping. The police sirens changed tone as they became closer. Each of the Russians broke free of the packages but had thick waterproof wrapping paper stuck to their hands. Dimitri tried to handle his pistol but dropped it. Boris looked at his two compatriots and also tried to grasp his pistol but was having a hard time of it too. Scott almost laughed but knew full well that this folly could turn to immediate danger.

"Boris, Vitali we must go. We'll have no time to escape if we stay any longer," Dimitri urged.

"The police will be here very shortly and we don't have enough firepower to take them on."

Boris looked at his comrades and the piles of neatly wrapped drug packages. He was sweating profusely and was visibly shaken.

"Grab what you can and deliver our last message to the Boy Scouts before we go," Vitali said.

He had thick, greasy paper stuck over his hands as he picked up four packages. Dimitri and Boris each picked up three packages and started walking quickly towards the front gates. Dimitri pulled out his pistol and forced his hand around the grip. He looked up at the verandah and fired two shots into the railing where Scott had been sitting. The large Russian then took aim at the fuel tank resting against the door and fired.

The bullets screamed through the railing, forcing small pieces of wood to fly everywhere before they lodged into the wall of the dome. Scott had already safely retreated inside and down towards the lighthouse keeper's desk the moment he threw the last package. The crack sound of the bullets and the small explosions they made caused Scott to flinch and hold his breath as he waited for something to find its mark closer to him. He folded his arms over his head when he heard the next shot.

The fuel tank did not explode. Dimitri's bullet pierced the tank, went through the fuel and out the other side before lodging itself into one of the thick, wooden doors. The sound of sirens and the sight of dust clouds along the dirt road leading to the jail stopped Dimitri firing another shot. He waved his weapon in the air and ran to join his comrades who were heading towards the hinterland where they had stashed their boat. The plan was for the three men to make their way to the highway and hitchhike back to Sydney.

The shooting stopped but the wail of police sirens filled the air. Scott made his way back to the verandah and peered over the railing towards the main jail outer gates. He glimpsed the three men entering the hinterland and saw a convoy of cars approaching the jail. Scott stood up and watched as the first car came into sight. He waved his hands excitedly as he realised rescue was at hand.

Constable Rugless was in the lead car. He had purposefully ordered the sirens be sounded and the cars driven with lights flashing. His thinking was that the noise and lights may scare off the Russians who he strongly believed were holding the Venturers captive. Constable Rugless positioned his car at an angle to the front gates and got out. He walked to the passenger side of the car and used his field glasses to scan the jail and lighthouse. A smile soon spread over his face when he saw Scott waving to him.

When Scott noticed the police officer looking at him he placed his left hand by his side and pointed with his right hand where the Russians had gone. Constable Rugless acknowledged Scott and waved to him. He put his field glasses down and raised his hands in the air like someone saying they don't know.

Scott quickly became amused at this and raised three fingers on his hand and again pointed in the direction of the hinterland. Constable Rugless joined his right index finger

163

and thumb and raised his hand in a sign of acknowledgement.

Two State police officers and the two Federal agents joined Constable Rugless at his car. They had watched the finger pointing and wanted to know what was happening.

"It looks like three people have escaped into the bush behind us," Constable Rugless said.

"How do you know that?" Agent Lomax asked.

"That kid on the verandah of the lighthouse signalled to me. I bet he's one of the missing Venturers," Constable Rugless said.

The police decided to verify first exactly what Scott had signalled. They drew their pistols and entered the jail forecourt and spread out as they made their way to the main jail wooden doors. A large pool of petrol was starting to stain the area and pieces of waterproof paper were littered near the doors.

Scott yelled out to the police and told them that the Russians had run off.

"Who are you?" Constable Rugless asked.

"I'm one of a group of Venturers taken hostage by the men and locked up in this place," Scott said.

"Where are the other Venturers?" Constable Rugless asked.

"They are locked in cells downstairs. They're okay, but you need to get the three Russians," Scott said.

"Shayne, look at this," Constable John Dwyer said as he pointed to the bullet hole in the fuel tank.

Constable Rugless looked at the tank and then craned his head upwards again and asked, "What's your name?"

"I'm Scott Morrow," the boy replied.

"Well Scott Morrow, you had better let us in, unless there is something else you need to tell me now?" Constable Rugless said.

"The Russians will have paper stuck to their hands. They also have ten packages of drugs ... or something," Scott said.

"Okay Scott, we're onto it. Come on down and let us in," Constable Rugless said.

Scott made his way to the trapdoor and worked it free. He then climbed down the ladder and started running down the stairs. The lad stopped at the two cells where his Venturers and Mike were held and yelled out.

"We're free! We're free!"

"Scott! Scott what's happening? Are you okay? We heard lots of shooting," Mike yelled back from his peephole.

Scott walked over to Mike and excitedly told him he was on his way to let the police into the jail and they soon would be out of their cells. A rousing cheer went up in both cells. Mike started it and all the Venturers joined in. A chant that echoed through the jail started rising up from the cells. Scott started losing it emotionally and he walked away. The Venturers had started singing out, "WELL DONE SCOTT! WELL DONE SCOTT!" He made his way back to the front doors, stood for a moment, and wiped his eyes.

Moments later, Scott had unlatched the doors. He stood looking at Constable Rugless who was still holding his pistol in his hand. Scott's eyes wandered to the pistol.

"It's okay, we're real. Are there any other Russians still here?" Constable Rugless asked.

"No, the three of them escaped into the bushland behind you, towards where they had a small boat," Scott said.

"It's okay Scott. By the look of this fuel tank they won't be going too far," Constable Rugless said.

The police officer extended his hand and shook the youth's hand with a firm grip.

"By the sound of all that singing it's time we met your fellow Venturers," Constable Rugless said as he started laughing.

"Anything to shut them up," Scott said.

Constable Dwyer followed behind and noticed the open office and boogie boards.

"Shayne, we should set up our next command post here with an observation area on the lighthouse verandah," Constable Dwyer said.

"Yes, you had also better get the Feds involved in this as they will surely need to talk to our Russian friends when they are tracked down," Constable Rugless said.

Scott showed Constable Rugless the cells where Mike and the others were kept. After a short discussion, Scott took Constable Rugless to the lighthouse verandah. They inspected where the pistol shots had been fired at Scott and they also had a look towards where the Russians were last seen running. Constable Rugless went to check on the correct time by viewing his mobile phone and he noticed he had full reception.

"Scott, you have to do me a favour," Constable Rugless said. "Turn that infernal siren off will you while I make some calls? Also, if you know how to stop the beam, then shut it off please."

Scott broke out into a huge grin and went inside and turned off the siren. He walked over to the main control area and switched off the lighthouse beam. Scott looked around the operations room one more time.

His eyes scanned the lighthouse keeper's desk and the machinery that comprised the control mechanism for the lighthouse beam and grinned. There were still two more things to do; remove the V-sign from the beam's housing and correctly fly the flag. Scott spoke with Constable Rugless and explained what he thought was outstanding, but Scott was told to leave these things just as they were so they could be photographed for evidence.

"We have the lighthouse keeper on his way with the keys to let your mates out of their cell. He won't be long. In regards to the Russians, suffice to say they are headed in a direction where there is no way out," Constable Rugless said.

It was over. At least for Scott and the Venturers.

CHAPTER THIRTY-FIVE

Admiral Ritchie replaced the receiver. He was told by Rear Admiral Curry that the Pushkin had been stopped by HMAS Eastralia and boarded by members of the SASR. The Captain and his crew had been taken captive and the Russian ship was being sailed back to Australia by Navy personnel.

The Federal government drove a media frenzy over the ensuing days about the vigilance of its armed forces and the operation that was used to capture the Pushkin. Selected photos of the SASR rappelling from a Seasprite onto the Pushkin and members of HMAS Eastralia and the Customs vessel, Lady Yvonne, were splashed over the front pages of most newspapers and led television and radio news bulletins for almost a week.

The New South Wales government was facing an election in a few months. They tried to capitalise through the media on how thorough the NSW police were in leading the chase for the drug-smuggling Russians and their leading role in the Russians eventual capture in bushland near Seal Rocks. The media went looking for heroes and found one in the shape of a blonde-haired, green-eyed teenager who took on the Russians and helped save his Venturer unit and its leader from certain death.

Scott was feted by the media with live interviews, feature stories and the suggestion of a film about his exploits. Throughout the media interview process, Scott made the point over and over again that what helped him the most was the great training his Venturer leader, Mike, had given him. He also lauded the camaraderie of his unit and said this bond of friendship had given him an extended family he never had before.

Major General Brian McGrath's voice boomed through the loudspeakers that were set up on the grassy forecourt of Government House. The change in tone and the increased volume brought Scott back from his daydream.

The General asked for Scott to come forward. Scott came to attention and marched out into the open forecourt and stopped a metre from the Governor. He saluted and the Governor returned the salute. Scott then went to the 'at ease' position.

"This is the day we pay special homage to a young man who helped save the lives of his entire Venturer unit, including his leader in a well-publicised event the Royal Australian Navy called Operation Stella," General McGrath said.

"Also, it is said a Queen's Scout is someone who places their training at the disposal of the community. I believe Scott has lived up to this, and more. With his prowess in helping thwart not one, but three, armed and highly dangerous aggressors Scott brought his unit's plight to the notice of the authorities," he said.

"The New South Wales government has decided to award Scott Morrow with the Conspicuous Bravery Medal. This is only the twenty-fifth time that this medal has been awarded since its gazettal in 1932."

"It is with great pleasure, and with the thanks of the government of New South Wales and the people of this state, I present you Scott, with this award. You have also completed your Queen's Scout in the intervening period and I also award you Scouting's highest youth honour," General McGrath added.

Scott stepped forward and received the awards. He stepped back and saluted the Governor. The media seemed to be everywhere as they focused on Scott. He bit his lip and tried to concentrate on the moment as he returned to his position among the recipient Venturers.

Mike was not through yet. He led his Venturers in another chorus of, "WELL DONE SCOTT! WELL DONE SCOTT!" The crowds picked up on the emotion and joined in the singing as well. The media went ballistic as they tried to capture the moment. While some members of Scott's unit held a banner high with the words, *Well Done Scott* printed on it, Mike and four of the Venturers broke with protocol. They formed up, marched onto the forecourt, and stopped next to Scott. They did a right turn to face him and then reached for the teenager and hoisted him up on to their shoulders.

The Governor stood in awe as the crowds went wild with spontaneous clapping and cheering at the youth. General McGrath looked at Scott and gave him the thumbs up.

Now it was over.